COUNTERPOINT

SHAY LACY

author of *Touchpoint*
and *Hero Needed*

CRIMSON
ROMANCE

F+W Media, Inc.

This edition published by
Crimson Romance
an imprint of F+W Media, Inc.
10151 Carver Road, Suite 200
Blue Ash, Ohio 45242
www.crimsonromance.com

Copyright © 2013 by Shay Lacy

ISBN 10: 1-4405-6211-3
ISBN 13: 978-1-4405-6211-2
eISBN 10: 1-4405-6212-1
eISBN 13: 978-1-4405-6212-9

Cover art © 123rf.com; istockphoto.com/jhorrocks

Thanks to the lawyers I know who love practicing law: Jillian Chantal and Elizabeth Vaughan.

Thanks to Maumee Valley RWA, for monthly goal setting, to the B-I-C group for online accountability and my fellow Panera Prison inmates, who take me away from housework to write. Special thanks to Ray Wenck, my critique partner, who spouts sense, and to my friends Constance Phillips and Jenna Rutland, who accompany me on my journeys both literal and imaginative. As always, my thanks to my husband, who encourages me to do what I love.

Prologue

Who sent this? Bryce Gannon wondered, as he turned over the thick brown padded envelope marked CONFIDENTIAL looking for the return address. But the criminal defense attorney found no clue. Did it contain something for a case? He worked at the tight seal with his letter opener, but just as his curiosity was about to be appeased his phone rang. With one hand he reached for it, his gaze shifting away from the envelope.

Boom. The envelope exploded, shooting white powder into the air, just missing Bryce's face. He jerked, dropping the envelope, which poofed another small cloud of white. What the hell . . . ? He inhaled and choked on the dust.

A letter bomb.

From the outer office he heard a woman's frightened scream. His desk phone continued to shrill for his attention.

God, a bomb. He coughed, trying to wave away the white mist, until his brain finally kicked in. *Get up, you fool. Get away from this crap.*

Ramming his chair back from his desk, he sprang clear of the cloud. But he continued to cough. His right hand was covered with white and tingled from the explosion's percussion. The powder, whatever it was, blended into his stark white shirt.

"Bryce!" his office manager Sharron Rudgate shrieked from the doorway, "Are you hurt?" Her eyes were wild.

"Call nine-one-one," he managed, although it took all his breath to get those four syllables out. He couldn't seem to draw enough air into his lungs.

5

Sharron shouted his message into the hall before stepping towards him, her hand outstretched. He waved her back. He didn't want anyone else inhaling this crap. A young researcher appeared behind Sharron, her face white as she stared at him.

There was an awful taste in his mouth, more bitter than chemical. He couldn't seem to clear his throat. God, was it poison?

"Bryce, how much of that did you breathe in?" The usually unruffled Sharron sounded nearly hysterical. "What is it?"

Bryce couldn't answer either question. He couldn't breathe. His lungs screamed for air. His bronchial tubes spasmed painfully. His breath whistled as he drew it in. He tore at his silk tie, undoing the knot, and yanked at the button of his linen shirt collar so hard the button snapped off. But it didn't help. He clutched his throat with one hand and his chest with the other. His lungs were on fire.

His knees buckled, dumping him to the plush carpet.

Jesus, he was going to die.

"Bryce!" Sharron screamed. "Bryce, oh my God!"

Bryce had no breath to speak. There were more frightened faces in the doorway standing at a safe distance listening to the sound of his tortured breathing. His staff, his office, his legal practice. The trappings of his success.

He saw his life pass before his eyes and felt deeply disappointed. He'd never been in love, never married, and never had children. He'd gotten criminals off on technicalities to roam free to hurt more people. He'd accepted large amounts of money from them, like the check with lots of zeroes on it he got today from accused racketeer Adam Steele. It was dirty money, guilty money—*blood* money. Thirty pieces of silver to betray himself and the law he loved. He'd had so much promise coming out of law school . . . and *this* was what his life amounted to. He knelt on the thick carpet like a supplicant, pleading for his miserable life.

He didn't think he'd be cashing that check.

Suffocating hurt. He'd scream at the pain if he could, but he couldn't. His heart pounded in his ears, laboring hard. Black spots danced before his eyes. His friends needed him. It was too bad Bryce would fail them at the end. He couldn't even pass on any messages to them. Dammit, he wanted to live. As his strength faded he sank to the carpet.

The world spun away with his regrets.

CHAPTER 1

Bryce Gannon should have been lying on a slab in the morgue. Instead, a ventilator kept the comatose defense attorney breathing, the thump and whoosh of the mechanical bellows and the monitoring equipment's rhythmic beep the only sounds in his suburban Detroit ICU room. He resembled a corpse except for the forced rise and fall of his bare chest and the bluish cast to his skin that marked his respiratory system's distress.

On the other side of the ICU glass, Ciara Alafita felt like a ghoulish voyeur. From what she'd heard of the impassive Gannon, she thought he'd hate this exposure and vulnerability. Well, as low as his blood pressure was, he might not yet survive whoever had tried to kill him so he could be embarrassed by his current condition.

She asked the man beside her, "Have the police found out who sent Gannon the letter bomb yet?"

Michigan State Attorney General Lawrence Baisden shook his head, his eyes detailing the scene inside the room. "I expect a report shortly." He was in his early fifties, tall, with a commanding presence.

"Ricin is a bio-terrorist poison. Why would a terrorist choose Gannon as his target? He defends criminals like them." Ciara had wondered why they'd driven an hour and a half from the state capital in Lansing to see Gannon in the hospital. She'd also wondered why the top man at the Attorney General's office had pulled her out of her department to accompany him.

"I don't think it was a terrorist attack," Baisden said. "I wonder if it's fallout from that mess with his friends last month." He nodded to the black-haired man who sat in a chair beside Gannon's bed.

Ciara recognized Paul Ziko, one of those friends, from the news. "But the real criminal confessed. Why would anybody target Gannon instead of him? Gannon defended the innocent party."

"Were the rest of Gannon's friends innocent? You must have seen the news, Ciara. Didn't you wonder why more people weren't arrested? I did. Maybe the victims' families did too."

Startled, Ciara turned away from the view of the man in the bed. "Are you suggesting a cover-up? One that Gannon engineered?"

Baisden's brown eyes pierced her. "I'm suggesting Gannon's so good at getting people out of legal jams that mobster Adam Steele hired him. I question Gannon's associations and I don't like the conclusions I'm drawing."

Ciara sucked in her breath in surprise and lowered her voice. "This is about Gannon being asked to run for judge, isn't it?"

Baisden nodded. "If he has poor judgment, or worse, I want to know about it now. I don't want someone corrupt on my team."

That's why the Attorney General had chosen her. Her department dealt with local elections and public offices. But it still didn't explain why he'd picked a junior lawyer in that department.

A nurse in brightly patterned scrubs hung another IV bag, attracting Ciara's attention again into the room.

"You may not have to worry about that."

"Gannon's a fighter. I think he's going to make it, but he'll need time to recover. Ricin poison is nasty stuff." His cell phone chimed quietly and he quickly grabbed it off his belt. "Excuse me." He turned aside to answer the call. "Baisden."

Ciara watched the nurse write vital information on Gannon's chart. Nobody deserved murder, not even cold-hearted reptiles like Gannon who defended murderers. And he had defended one innocent man recently, although it had probably been a fluke.

Cover-up or not, Paul Ziko's loyalty amazed her. She had no close friends who'd sit beside her bedside if she was ill or injured. Her family would, despite their differences. Which made her wonder why Gannon didn't have family by his side.

Baisden turned back to her. "That was the forensics report. There were no prints on the envelope. Whoever sent the letter bomb didn't want to get caught."

Ciara looked at the still figure violated with tubes and wires. "What about a jealous husband?" If Gannon had no scruples about whom he defended, maybe he lacked other scruples as well.

"No. Gannon recently broke up with Monique Dennison, the former Miss Michigan. She was runner-up for Miss USA. He dated her for the past year. She's single."

Ciara attached the name to a face—a stunning, statuesque blonde. Pageant queens could be cutthroat. "Maybe she's the bomber, a woman scorned and all that."

"The newspapers said she ended it."

"So the bomber could be anybody. And you think something Gannon is or was involved in made someone decide to kill him?"

"Definitely. I want you to find out what he's mixed up with."

"Me? How?" She was a paper pusher, not an investigator.

"He'll need help while he recovers."

"I'm not a nurse or a therapist."

"Legal help. You've got your law degree. So work for him. Find out how compromised he is and report back to me. If I'm right, I'll nip his aspirations in the bud. I won't have a fool or someone corrupt on the bench."

"So he won't know I'm with the Attorney General's office?"

"No. You can tell him you're moving home to be closer to your sick father."

Ciara gave Baisden a sharp glance. Her heart skipped a beat. Did he know she was estranged from her father? She wouldn't put it past him. The AG had his ear to all kinds of grapevines.

"How long do you think it will take?" she asked carefully. The thought of moving back to her hometown for an extended period disturbed her. Her fingers curled against the cool surface of the ICU window.

"If you're lucky, a week," Baisden replied. "If not, you have until Steele's trial starts in two weeks."

Ciara faced him. "Why me? I don't report directly to you. You've got more experienced people who do."

"You've got brains and beauty, Ciara, a combination that could take you far. I've discussed your future with your supervisor several times. He said you've got great potential . . . except for that big chip on your shoulder about men. Your first two suggestions about suspects showed you didn't think much of men. My office is political, Ciara. We can't afford to offend half the people who vote us there."

Ciara reined in her hurt, although she trembled with the injustice of it. Baisden didn't think much of Gannon himself. "So you think proving Bryce Gannon is a fool or corrupt will knock that chip off my shoulder?"

"Not all men are bad, Ciara. You're painting us all with the same brush. Maybe you had a bad experience with a man or a string of bad experiences. I don't know and I don't care. I do care that it makes you less of an asset to my office. Take this time to figure out which is which, and give me an unbiased report on Gannon."

He glanced into the ICU room again. His lips tightened, he shook his head and walked away.

Ciara looked one last time. The respirator still whooshed and thumped with every mechanical breath. The monitors still beeped every slow heartbeat. Bryce Gannon continued to lie immobile as the doctors fought the ricin damage.

She had no illusions she could lie well to Gannon or that she could win him over with her looks. Baisden had said she had brains and beauty, but in her experience men didn't want brains—they wanted big boobs. That wasn't her. Her intelligence intimidated men and had since high school. And men wanted blondes, while she was Latina. Gannon had just spent a year with a gorgeous, buxom blonde. How could Ciara get him to believe her story when she was the antithesis of the beauty queen?

Ciara's hands curled into fists. She entertained no fantasies about her feminine charms either. Her parents had reproached her often enough about her unfeminine choices—playing basketball and practicing law. She'd come out on the losing end when they compared her to her more traditional sister who was a housewife and mother.

She exhaled her frustration. It didn't matter how she got close to Gannon. Baisden had subtly warned her that her position in his office was in jeopardy if she didn't change the way she felt about men. She needed this job. Part of every paycheck went to her sister so their mother could live with her.

She shivered in the air conditioning, feeling cold all the way through. Baisden thought spying on Gannon—a man he didn't trust—would change Ciara. It certainly would. She'd have to become the thing she despised most—a liar and a cheat. She'd have to become just like her father.

• • •

"What happened?" Bryce rasped. He woke confused—his throat sore, his chest tight, and his lungs on fire—to find his best friends surrounding him. He lay flat on his back on something soft. The light was too bright and he felt cold.

"You're in the hospital, Bryce," his University of Michigan fraternity brother Dr. Sean Bergman explained, laying a warm hand on Bryce's shoulder. "It was a letter bomb."

Sean's short brown hair was liberally salted with gray. Worry filled his brown eyes. He wore a suit, which meant it was a weekday.

Bryce remembered now. The boom. The spray of white powder. Coughing, choking, collapsing to the carpet in his office unable to breathe, desperate for air, sure he was dying, and then nothing. But he'd survived. Joy and relief made him feel dizzy.

Then he recalled the envelope with no return address on it. "Who sent it?"

Sean cleared his throat. "The cops don't know." A trace of uneasiness laced his voice.

Roger Barrett added, "The police are waiting to hear you're awake. They've already talked to us, but we didn't know anything that could help them. We thought maybe you'd know."

Bryce shook his head. "I don't have any enemies." His voice sounded gravelly.

Sean shared a glance with their other two fraternity brothers. Roger looked haggard, with dark circles under his eyes, gaunt cheeks, and his artfully streaked blonde hair dulled. A faltering architectural firm and a son in jail were taking their toll on him.

The strain lines in Paul Ziko's face were new, caused by his struggling construction company and his pending divorce.

Sean had mishandled a patient's medical care. As a result, his easy smile was absent.

The four of them had achieved the American dream of success—a doctor, a lawyer, an architect, and a business developer. But their perfect lives were coming undone. Even his.

Bryce already felt like shit physically. Now he'd dumped more stress on his friends when they were fighting for their survival. A quick inventory told him he had all his fingers. His bare chest showed no wounds. His face?

White powder exploding. "What was in that bomb?"

"Ricin poison," Sean answered.

"Ricin." Bryce couldn't remember what he'd heard about ricin.

"It's made from castor beans. It's highly toxic." Sean swallowed. Bryce's friends looked uneasy. "Someone meant to kill you."

God. "The phone rang while I was opening it and I looked away."

"That saved your life," Paul said, his voice thick.

Bryce ran a hand over his bare chest. "My chest hurts, but I don't see any wounds."

Sean pressed his arm. "That's the ricin poisoning. It can cause respiratory and circulatory problems, coughing, weakness, fever, nausea, and muscle aches. Your skin was blue for the first few days, but that's faded now."

Bryce looked down to find his chest and arms flesh-colored. "Days?" he croaked. "How long since the bomb?"

"It's been three days, Bryce," Roger answered. "We've been with you the whole time. I was so glad when Sean called to say you were finally coming around."

Bryce had lost three days . . . and almost lost his life. His throat thickened and his chest tightened painfully. Despite their own troubles, his friends had come to him in his hour of need, just as they had in college during a nearly lethal hazing.

Afterwards they'd become his friends and his armor until he devised his own. Over the years he'd perfected a cold exterior that repelled predators. He never intended to be that vulnerable again. The four of them were tarnished now—they'd made mistakes—but they stuck together. Their friendship was the most valuable thing he'd gained in college.

"Thanks for being here, guys." His rasp was getting worse.

Sean gripped Bryce's hand. "You would have done the same for one of us."

"*Have* done the same for us," Paul corrected.

"I'm glad you survived," Roger added, his voice tight and his light-colored eyes suspiciously moist.

"Me too." Bryce squeezed Sean's hand.

Roger took hold of his other hand, careful around the wires and tubes.

If four battered men could find something good out of this catastrophe, it was a miracle. Before the bomb Bryce had begun to wonder if his life had gotten off track somewhere. Clearly, if someone wanted to kill him, he was on a path he didn't want to tread. This was a wake-up call for Bryce to climb out of the gutter of criminals and get back to why he became a lawyer.

He gripped his friends' hands. He'd sworn friendship with these men, and twenty years later he still upheld that oath. It was a place to start finding his way back to himself.

A tall, slender brunette in patterned scrubs bustled into the room, nodding at his friends. "Hi, I'm Marilyn. I'm your day nurse. I'm glad you're awake at last, Mr. Gannon. How do you feel?"

Roger moved aside and she took his place, gripping Bryce's wrist at the pulse point.

"Lousy." Bryce had to strain for the next breath. "When can I get out of here?"

Marilyn made a notation on his chart and uncoiled her stethoscope from around her neck. "It's like that, is it?" She tucked the earpieces into her ears and placed the cold end against his chest. He jerked.

After a minute she removed the stethoscope, and made another notation. "Is it hard to breathe?"

He nodded, frustrated.

Then to his mortification she slipped an oxygen mask over his face. Past her, he saw his friends' concerned faces.

"The greater oxygen flow will help. I'm sure the doctor will order a breathing treatment soon that will make it easier to breathe. And to answer your question, now that you're awake you'll probably be moved to a regular room."

That wasn't what he'd meant by leaving.

"When will you know for sure?" Sean asked.

"I'll page Dr. Robbins now. But he probably won't be here for a few hours. I can call you afterwards, Dr. Bergman." Marilyn glanced quickly at Bryce. "If that's all right with you, Mr. Gannon."

Bryce nodded. If the hospital was according Sean professional courtesy, all the better for Bryce. Sean could sort through the crap and evasions and medicalese, and then tell Bryce the truth. He sorely needed truth now.

But he needed something else almost as much. He hated being stripped of his physical armor. His emotional armor didn't bear thinking about. He at least wanted to be clothed.

Bryce took a deep breath and pulled off the oxygen mask. "I need clothes," he told his friends.

"You won't need anything yet," Marilyn corrected him. "Except rest. So I'm going to have to ask your friends to leave."

She didn't understand. She hadn't spent her adult life building a protective shell to prevent people from hurting her. He had.

He looked Paul in the eye. "Bring me my clothes." Paul would understand. He'd known Bryce needed help during the hazing.

Paul nodded. "Something casual coming up." He glanced at Sean. "You'll let me know?"

"Yeah. I'll let all of you know."

Sean squeezed Bryce's hand. "I've got patients, but I'll be back to see you later. I'll bring you information on ricin."

Bryce squeezed back and nodded.

"I'm glad you're awake. Your doctor will probably run tests to determine if there's any permanent damage."

God, permanent damage? Bryce's heart pounded hard and his chest tightened even more painfully. The monitor's beeps quickened to match his heartbeat.

Marilyn frowned at it and then at his friends. "Gentlemen."

"We can talk about all that later," Sean promised. "We're here for you, Bryce."

"Thanks," Bryce croaked, glancing from Sean to the others.

Sean stepped away and Roger took his place. "Now that you're awake, I need to get back to the office. I've left Christian and Gabrielle to run the business. I think they'll appreciate some newlywed time today."

Paul gripped Roger's shoulder as he stared down at Bryce. Paul and Roger had the strongest connection. They worked in the same industry and Paul's brother Christian was Roger's business partner. In a way, Bryce envied their closeness. These men were the only true friends he'd ever had; yet even with them he still felt separate. Not an outsider, not with them. Just emotionally distant.

Had a childhood with emotionally distant parents and an adulthood fortifying emotional walls around him made it impossible for him to share what Paul and Roger did? And if he wanted closeness like that, could he let down his walls? The question bothered him.

CHAPTER 2

Later that afternoon Bryce tried to get comfortable in his hospital bed in his private room. He'd had two breathing treatments since that morning and a battery of tests. His chest ached, his lungs burned, and he felt exhausted even though he hadn't done anything strenuous. He wanted to lie flat but his doctor was allegedly due at any moment and he intended to face the man from a position of strength. Never let the other guy see vulnerability. He'd learned that lesson well.

He needed to get out of here and in order to do that he had to convince his doctor he was well. Damn this weakness. At least they'd given him a hospital gown. He ran his palm down his chest feeling the well-laundered cotton, not the fine starched linen or silk he usually wore. His hand brushed the EKG leads and he grimaced, looking up to where the monitor displayed his vital signs for anyone to see. He still felt exposed.

Instead of an oxygen mask, he wore a thin nasal cannula. He hated it, hated what it told other people about his condition.

A knock preceded his personal physician, Dr. Marc Robbins, and the pulmonologist he'd met today, Dr. Hany Khalil. Robbins was forty-two, dark-haired, and trim. Bryce had met him at his gym and liked the other man's drive. Dr. Khalil was in his fifties, his graying dark hair looked distinguished against his swarthy skin. Both men wore serious expressions. Not good.

Bryce braced himself. Pain shot through his chest.

"Bryce." Dr. Robbins gripped his hand, brief but firm. Bryce had liked that about the man. "Don't talk too much. We know you're worn out from the tests."

How the hell did they know that? Bryce had thought he'd managed a cool façade of languorous ease, despite the unsightly gown.

"Mr. Gannon," Dr. Khalil spoke briskly with an accent. "I have analyzed your test results. You've lost thirty-seven percent of your lung capacity."

God. No wonder it was hard to breathe.

"I'm afraid the damage is irreparable. There's scarring in the lung tissue already."

Bryce tried to control rising panic. *Irreparable damage.* He tried to calm his breathing, but the monitor betrayed him.

Dr. Khalil continued with his efficient onslaught. "What this means for you is that you'll experience shortness of breath, especially with exercise, possibly wheezing, coughing, and chest tightness."

"Bryce," Dr. Robbins added, "You probably won't be able to run anymore."

God. He'd run track since boarding school. He prided himself on being fit and fast. Now, because of some sick bastard, he was going to be benched. He pressed his lips together to keep from blistering the air with curses.

Dr. Khalil took up the account once more. "I'll prescribe a bronchodilator—an inhaler—to relax your lung muscles. It'll make breathing easier."

"Like an asthma inhaler?" Bryce croaked. There was no strength in his voice.

Dr. Khalil nodded. "Yes, like that. You'll have a long-acting bronchodilator for the first few months."

Months.

"And a short-acting one for periods of stress."

God, two drugs when he'd never had to take any. Bryce saw Dr. Robbins more at the gym than he did in his medical office. They were on a first-name basis.

"You'll need pulmonary rehab . . . " Dr. Khalil continued.

"Rehab?" Like drug rehab? God, no. He wasn't staying here for that.

"Breathing exercises with a respiratory therapist."

Now they thought he had to be taught how to breathe. Bryce would have laughed or scoffed if he'd had the breath.

"And you'll have a portable oxygen tank."

The rest of Dr. Khalil's words faded at the vision of Bryce in court wearing oxygen. He'd seen people with them and pitied them. His fist tightened. That wouldn't be *him*.

"No oxygen tank," he growled. He would not be pitied— worse, scorned—or made a target to be victimized.

"For emergencies, Bryce," Marc explained. "For when you've overexerted or for ozone action days, things like that. At first, you'll need it daily, but gradually you'll need the oxygen less and less."

It was suddenly too much to take. Despite his years of training as a lawyer, Bryce turned away from the doctors—a sign of weakness in itself. His eyes burned. He would not disgrace himself.

In a way, the letter bomb had crippled him, robbed him of his perfect health and his perfect control. It had made him less than he'd been, now drug dependent. Drugs were for weak people. He was strong . . . had been strong. His body had been pure—no cigarettes, no illegal drugs, no tattoos—just healthy and fit. He was thirty-nine years old and had looked forward to turning forty this fall in good shape.

"Bryce, I know it's hard to accept right now," Marc tried to soothe. "But you're alive. The ricin could easily have killed you. This is a small hardship when you think of it that way."

A small hardship. Right. Robbins wouldn't be saying that if *he* were the one lying in this bed. Bryce turned back to them; his anger and bitterness helping him control his other feelings once more.

"Thanks, doctors."

"If you need to talk to a professional about this—" Marc began.

"I have Sean Bergman," Bryce interrupted in a rasp.

Dr. Robbins brightened. "That's right, he's a psychiatrist. Do you want him updated on today's findings? You were unconscious when you were admitted, so we gave Dr. Bergman professional courtesy as your friend."

"Please update him." Bryce wet his dry lips and breathed in some oxygen. "When can I go home?"

Marc frowned at him. "Bryce, you nearly died. You were unconscious for three days. You couldn't walk as far as the door right now if you wanted to. You're going to be in here at least a week."

A week. "I'm due in court."

"I heard you're defending Adam Steele." Marc's lips pursed in disapproval. "You might want to turn your cases over to an associate."

Bryce frowned and shifted with discomfort. He had no associates. He'd been a star attorney for years. All he had was a staff of assistants, researchers mostly.

Robbins must have read Bryce's resistance in his expression. "Bryce, this is your life we're talking about. If you don't take the time to recuperate, you may not get your strength back."

Bryce drilled Marc with a glare. There was no way he'd want to stay in this condition. Malingering wasn't his thing.

The other doctor took Bryce's silence for assent. "I'll put together your rehab plan and go over it with you tomorrow." He turned towards the door.

Marc gripped Bryce's arm briefly. "Save your energy for the fight to get better and let the hospital staff take care of you. I'll see you tomorrow."

Then Bryce was alone, just him and his debilitation. Against Marc's advice, he swung his legs over the side of the bed. Runner's legs with smoothly muscled calves and thighs. He couldn't accept that he wouldn't run again. He gathered his strength and pushed himself to a standing position, then gripped the cold metal bed rail for support when his legs trembled. His chest and lungs ached from that single exertion.

He firmed his stance and forced his fingers to let go of the rail. Belatedly, tugs on his body made him remember he was tied to the monitors, the IV pole, and the oxygen. With a yank he ripped the monitor leads from his chest enduring the sharp pain of uprooted chest hair. The monitor squawked an alarm in an annoying blare. He lifted the oxygen tube over his head, gripped the smooth metal of the wheeled IV pole, and forced one foot in front of the other. He could do this. The doctors were wrong. He didn't have permanent lung damage. He moved the next foot, then the other again. He'd show them he didn't need rehab.

Sweat beaded on his forehead. His breaths were shallow and he couldn't seem to make them deeper.

Two more steps brought him closer to the door. The waxed floor was cool against his bare feet. He wondered where his five hundred dollar, hand-stitched Italian leather shoes were.

His vision seemed hazy at the edges. He focused desperately on the chair closest to the door as a midpoint. His breath burned in his lungs as it did when he sprinted. See, this was nothing new. The doctors didn't know what they were talking about.

The door burst inward and a woman in white scrubs nearly plowed into him. Her wide eyes took him in as he reached for the chair.

"Mr. Gannon, what are you doing out of bed?"

Someone else entered behind her, but Bryce couldn't see who it was. He seemed to be sinking. It was all he could do to control the downward motion towards the chair. With relief he sank onto the seat. His breath whistled in and out. His chest felt like an iron band constricted it.

Bryce tried to tell her some facile lie, but he couldn't get breath to speak.

"Get the portable oxygen tank," the nurse said to whoever was behind her.

Bryce didn't need the damn oxygen. He tried to wave her off but she gripped his wrist. Probing for his pulse, he finally realized. He couldn't shake her loose.

The other staff member—a stocky, dark-haired man—slipped an oxygen mask over Bryce's nose and mouth. Bryce wanted to growl and rant at them, but the sweet rush of oxygen cooled the burning in his lungs.

"Just relax and inhale," the nurse instructed, releasing his wrist at last.

They both looked at him like he'd been a bad boy, when all he'd wanted was to take back control of his life. God, he couldn't even cross a room without getting winded, just as Marc had predicted.

"Are you feeling better?" Her nametag read Nancie.

Bryce nodded.

"You're not supposed to be up and around yet. You're that fancy lawyer who's going to defend that mobster." Again he heard the hint of disapproval. "Well in the courtroom you might be king, but here you do as the doctor orders and he wants bed rest."

He had other battles to fight and at the moment he'd used up what little energy he had. His body shook with the effort he'd expended.

Bryce let them help him back to bed, hating to admit how much he needed their assistance.

Sometime later the phone's jangle roused him from a doze. He reached automatically for it and had it in his hand before he remembered where he was.

"Gannon," he croaked.

"Mr. Gannon, it's Adam Steele. I'm so glad to hear your voice. I was worried when I heard about the letter bomb."

Yeah, worried about whether he'd get off on the federal racketeering charges. Here was the perfect opportunity to drop the suspected mobster's case.

"They tell me I have lung damage. I'll be awhile recovering." Bryce didn't have to fake his gasping breath. "I recommend you find another lawyer."

"I'm sure the judge will understand our request for a delay. I'm happy with the lawyer I have. So you'll stay on the case."

Anger spurted through Bryce. The man didn't seem to care that Bryce's recovery might take months—not that he intended for it to. "I can't say whether I'll practice defense law when I get well."

"Mr. Gannon, you thrive against an opponent. You and I are alike in that respect. And we're very successful at it. I need the best defending me, Mr. Gannon, and you're it. There's no question you'll defend me. None at all."

"I understand your day nurse is Nancie. Is she taking good care of you?"

Bryce's heart stuttered. My God, Steele had a pipeline into the hospital.

"I'd hate for you to have any painful setbacks in your care. I'm very interested in your treatments so you'll have a speedy recovery. I'd really like for you to recover."

The veiled threat made Bryce's breath stop. Right now he couldn't run, he couldn't hide, and he could only protect himself one way.

"I understand, Mr. Steele."

"I knew you would. And after you get me out of my little legal jam, I'll see to it you get that judgeship you were thinking about.

It would be mutually beneficial to have a friend on the bench, don't you agree?"

"I can see that it would." Bryce's voice was fading.

"I'm tiring you when I want just the opposite. Please don't worry about anything but getting well. I'll be interested in updates on your condition, and when you're ready to get back to work, I'll help in any way possible."

"Thanks."

Steele said good-bye and Bryce dropped the phone back into the cradle. As he lay back against the pillow, a huge weight settled on him. He'd have to defend a man he thought was guilty and get the man acquitted so Steele could continue his mob activities. Bryce could do it. He'd done it dozens of times before. But he didn't want to this time.

The only way to reclaim his younger, less contaminated self was to steer clear of the Adam Steeles of this world. But Steele had made it plain what would happen if Bryce did. And a connection to Steele now would become a life-long connection.

Bryce groaned. What the ricin had begun, Steele would finish. For a second Bryce wondered if Steele had sent the letter bomb. Had Bryce tipped his hand that he was thinking about abandoning the case? No, ricin was too lethal a substance to be certain of attaining Bryce's cooperation without accidentally killing him.

No, Steele wanted him alive and in court. At least Steele wanted him alive—for now.

Bryce closed his eyes. His future looked pretty bleak at the moment.

• • •

Bryce should have been used to cops by now, but he'd never been a victim before—well, not that the cops knew about. He hadn't reported the hazing incident. These Feds were investigating the federal crime of the letter bomb. He was glad Sean had brought his clothes. Dressed in a navy blue jogging suit and with an afternoon nap and hours of oxygen behind him, Bryce felt armored enough to deal with FBI agents Garrison and Pollack. Garrison reminded him of a street fighter, all dark and wiry. Pollack was stick straight, dirty blonde, and bland.

They'd questioned Bryce about everyone he knew to figure out who might've sent him the letter bomb. He just didn't understand why he'd been the target. He told them he'd received no threatening letters or phone calls.

"I'm a defense attorney." Bryce sucked in needed air. "And I usually win. My former clients have no reason to hurt me."

"You're defending Adam Steele," Garrison said, referring to his notebook. "Are you aware someone's making a move on his organization?"

Bryce stilled. "No." The idea chilled him. Had he been the victim of a power play, just a pawn to be disposed of?

"It's not common knowledge," Garrison continued. "And we want it to stay in this room. Our FBI sources tell us someone would like to step into Steele's shoes and they suggest it's someone inside his organization. Maybe putting his attorney out of commission would assure Steele went to jail."

"Too indirect," Bryce argued.

"Not if the rival wanted to be subtle," Garrison suggested. "It's death in that organization to announce your opposition openly."

"Anyone been following you, any strange cars or people?" Pollack quizzed, the blandness absent from his tone.

"No."

"Ex-wives, ex-girlfriends, ex-lovers?" Garrison asked.

"I recently broke up with Monique Dennison," Bryce said. "We'd been together a year."

Garrison's eyes widened. "She's the former Miss Michigan." His look questioned Bryce's sanity over the break-up.

"She broke it off. We wanted different things." Bryce had told her he was thinking about giving up his lucrative law practice to become a judge and she'd walked away. He didn't miss her. He hadn't thought of her once since he'd woken.

At one point he'd considered marrying her. They'd have a marriage like his parents had had—a successful husband, his wife the perfect social hostess, beautiful and gracious. She'd volunteer for charities and give him a child or two. They'd be comfortable. They'd have the same goals. Bryce's relationship with Monique had been just as loveless as his parents' marriage. He shuddered thinking about it now.

"Any other exes?" Pollack prodded.

Bryce shook his head. Sean handed him ice water and he gratefully sipped from the straw, although his hands chilled quickly. He and Sean were the bachelors of their group. He grimaced. Paul Ziko would become one too as soon as his divorce became final.

"Any negativity about the possibility of you running for judge?"

"No." Bryce had been a media darling after the Ziko affair. He wondered what he was now.

"Any fallout from the Christian Ziko case?"

Bryce shared a glance with Sean as he gave the cup back. "No." Except the restless certainty that something was wrong with his life.

"Any fan mail, any love letters?"

Bryce shook his head. Then he posed a question of his own. "Ricin is a bio-terrorist agent. Why use it on me?"

Sean cleared his throat. "Actually, Bryce, you can buy castor beans to make ricin over the Internet. The poison is easy to make, so anyone can do it."

"And you can find instructions on how to make letter bombs on the Internet too," Garrison agreed.

"So it wasn't terrorism?" Bryce insisted.

"We don't know for sure, although no group has claimed responsibility. We'll need a list of your cases, both open and shut, from the past year. We'll want to look for suspects there."

"Confidentiality," Bryce reminded them.

His early spurt of energy was fading and it was getting harder to breathe again. His gaze clashed with Sean's, who indicated the oxygen. Bryce shook his head. He wanted to appear strong for the remainder of this interview.

"Mr. Gannon," Pollack appealed, "Something in one of those cases may have triggered the attack. Your attacker is still out there. Do you want him or her to get a second chance at you?"

My God, Bryce hadn't thought of that. His heart galloped as the terror he'd felt the day of the poisoning replayed in his mind.

Sean stiffened from his casual pose. "Do you think that's likely, Agent Pollack?" His tone was sharp, his expression concerned.

The FBI agents exchanged glances and Garrison replied with care, "We don't know."

"Then why doesn't Bryce have police protection?" Sean demanded as his brows beetled in a furious frown.

"We thought he was safe enough in the ICU—" Pollack began.

Only to have Sean snap, "Where he was unconscious and completely defenseless against a second attack. I saw strangers in the ICU every day. One of them might have been the bomber."

Although Bryce appreciated his friend's defense, he hated the picture Sean painted of him as vulnerable. He'd expended a lot of energy to fool these FBI agents about his real condition.

Besides that, Bryce wasn't sure he wanted cops hovering around him every minute, especially while he worked on Steele's defense, or pretended to. Steele probably owned people in all levels of law enforcement, which would explain how he'd gotten away with criminal activity for years.

A tremor ran through Bryce as Sean and the Feds argued above him. Bryce already thought most, if not all, his clients, were lying to him. Now he had to wonder who might be on Steele's payroll, like whom here at the hospital was Steele's spy. He watched the pulse display as he breathed through his nose and tried to restore his calm.

"No cops," Bryce finally interrupted the argument.

"Bryce, he or she might try again," Sean argued.

"No cops, Sean."

Bryce would have enough strangers and interruptions in his life for the next few weeks, enough people dictating what he could and couldn't do. He wouldn't let anyone else confine him.

Sean's face set mulishly.

With a spurt of guilt, Bryce ignored his friend and addressed the Feds. "I'll give you restricted access to my client files. I'll call my office manager tomorrow to clear you. I won't let you take files out of my office." His voice slowly dropped in volume.

Now Garrison and Pollack looked mulish. Bryce didn't care. On this he would stand firm. He'd built a reputation of clients being able to trust their lives in his hands. They trusted him with confidential facts as well. He wouldn't lose that.

The Feds left and Bryce allowed Sean to badger him back into the oxygen. Sean lowered the bed's head so Bryce could lie down. As he relaxed into the not quite comfortable mattress, Sean pulled up a chair to discuss the doctors' diagnosis and what it meant to Bryce in brutally frank terms.

But even with Sean, Bryce didn't feel comfortable enough to let his fear and despair show.

CHAPTER 3

The next morning the sound of a footstep tore Bryce's attention from the Steele case file in his hands. A beautiful woman stood in his hospital room doorway. She was very tall and toned, athletic if he had to guess, but not a runner. A quick frown pulled her sleek black brows together, but it smoothed as she caught him staring.

"Mr. Gannon, you're working." Her voice was a pleasant contralto with a hint of accent.

She had the advantage over him. He closed the file. "Can I help you?" His voice was still hoarse today.

"I'm Ciara Alafita. Your office manager told me to bring you some reference books."

He must have looked blank, because she continued, "I'm your new legal assistant."

Legal assistant his ass. She was a model, maybe a reporter. That black knit top and black A-line skirt hinted at subtle feminine curves. He'd guess she was at least five foot ten. Her riotously curly black hair was pulled back from her face and most of it confined behind her head, exposing a bone structure women paid plastic surgeons to get. But he was certain this woman had been born with it. The bright red lips were made for kissing. Her name, dark brown eyes, and genetically tanned skin proclaimed her Latina.

Ruthlessly Bryce squelched his male interest. "You don't work for me."

She strode forward with confidence and a slight lift of her chin. "I was hired yesterday. As low man—or in my case, woman—on the totem pole, I get to do your legal research."

Yesterday he'd talked to Steele, who'd said he'd keep an eye on the case. Today Bryce had a beautiful new legal assistant. His belly went cold and his muscles tightened, making his chest ache.

"What's your background?" he asked.

"I worked in the Attorney General's office, but I missed my family, so I moved back to the Detroit area to be closer to them. I graduated second in my law class from the University of Michigan and I passed the bar exam. Lately I've been with the Opinions and Municipal Affairs Division at the AG."

My God, Steele had reach. The AG's office. Bryce's pounding heart made him feel sick. Steele had given her a poignant story—homesickness—but Bryce didn't believe it for a minute. People didn't abandon good jobs like that for the reason she'd stated. She was lying.

"I didn't know my office was hiring."

"They weren't. But I'm obviously overqualified and willing to work for less money, so they snapped me up." All said very coolly.

"One wonders why you'd do that?" he mused.

"I told you. My family—"

Bryce interrupted with a wave of his hand. "Why *my* office?"

"Your success rate is extraordinary. Why would I work for a less successful attorney?"

Why indeed? Again he sensed the lie. If her family had lived here all along, why miss them now? She'd been out of law school for some time. There was no such thing as coincidence.

"Would you step out of the room for a few minutes please," he ordered.

That rocked her composure. "Why?" The word quavered.

"I'm confined to bed. I need the nurse for personal reasons. You understand." He used the veiled crudeness on purpose.

She actually blushed. It was quaint. He quickly hardened himself against reacting to her.

As soon as she left, Bryce buzzed for the nurse. That would allay Ciara's suspicions. Then he called his office and asked for his office manager.

"It's Bryce. Did you hire someone?"

"You gave me hiring discretion," Sharron answered. "I take it she's there?"

"Describe her."

"Ciara Alafita, Hispanic, aged thirty-two, very tall, dark hair and eyes, she came from the AG's office. She's passed the bar. Is there a problem, Bryce? I know she's overqualified for the job."

"Why did you send her here?"

Sharron sighed. "Bryce, you nearly died. It's way too soon for you to be working. I know I can't stop you from overexerting, but I thought I'd send you the highest qualified person we have to help you prepare for the Steele case. At the moment, that's her."

So Steele had investigated the skill level in Bryce's office and sent someone better. Now the question was should Bryce send Ciara away? If he did, would Steele send someone else and take Ciara's dismissal as a negative sign?

"Bryce?" Sharron prompted.

An old adage came to Bryce's mind. Keep your friends close and your enemies closer. "I'll see how she works out, but for the time being I approve any hiring decisions and you ask me before you send a stranger to me."

Sharron sucked in her breath. "Bryce. Omigod, Bryce, she's not the bomber. She can't be. She came from the AG's office. I verified her references. I spoke to her former supervisor myself. He praised her work and was sorry to lose her."

Bryce felt like a paranoid fool, but better a paranoid fool than a dead one. "I'm just being careful, Sharron. Whoever attacked me is still out there."

"You'd be safer with police protection," she retorted.

"Thanks for your concern. I'll call you later."

"Bryce," Sharron nearly shrieked.

"Yes?"

"Are you feeling better today? You sound better than last night." In the four years she'd worked for him, he'd never gotten personal with Sharron. Of course, a near-fatal accident tended to change things.

"It's a little easier to breathe today, and they've still got me on oxygen." Although he wasn't wearing it at the moment and could tell. He shifted in bed, uncomfortable crossing the boss-employee line he'd set. To his intense relief, the nurse's appearance in his room gave him an out.

"The nurse is here. I have to go, Sharron."

When the nurse finished with him, he suffered through all the vital checks and she glared as she put his nasal cannula back on. He lay quietly through her lecture about how he was not to remove the oxygen.

As soon as she left, Ciara returned to the room. His heart speeded up again at her dark beauty, which led to yet another thought about Steele's shrewdness. Steele believed a beautiful woman could deceive Bryce. He was wrong. Bryce had just spent a year with an incredibly beautiful woman and had never once lost his head. He wouldn't become some lovestruck fool over Ciara.

• • •

Ciara watched the male appreciation in Bryce's blue eyes cool to ice. For a moment his approval had warmed her. She got that if men looked at her face first. If they looked at her chest, she saw their disappointment. But she'd never been frozen out. She pressed her lips together. She wasn't here to win Gannon's heart. She was here to do a job.

Bryce Gannon was known for his icy detachment, his cool exterior, and his iron control over his emotions. She'd spent the past few days learning all she could about him and studying his trials that had been filmed. Right now he was wearing his courtroom face.

She hadn't expected a warm welcome, not while he was so ill, but she hadn't expected his initial suspicion either. Although if some unknown person had tried to kill her, she might be suspicious of strangers too.

Ciara certainly hadn't expected Bryce to be dressed in sweats and sitting upright with case files on his hospital bed. Two days ago, he'd looked like a corpse. This was only his second day awake. He should be recuperating and resting in this private room.

A pang of guilt shot through her that she was aiding and abetting his flagrant disregard of the reason he was here. It pulsed with the other guilt about lying to him. She tried to dismiss her feelings, but was only partially successful. The sooner she completed her assignment, the sooner she could go back to the AG's office, and the sooner she could stop lying. Her assignment required Bryce working and interacting with Steele.

"Where do you want the books I brought?" Ciara walked towards the bed, noticing that he now wore a thin oxygen tube. His jacket zipper had been lowered and she could see the golden blonde chest hair beneath. It was lighter than the hair on his head, which was probably dulled from lack of washing.

Her heartbeat sped with excitement and her face warmed. She covered her heated reaction to ogling his body by stooping to her briefcase and reaching inside. In the few moments it took to retrieve the books, she had control of her face and body once more. She'd already seen Bryce naked from the waist up in the ICU, so why it was more intimate to glimpse his body under his clothes defied logic.

Bryce was good-looking in a ruggedly elegant way. She could admit that. Not too pretty, yet not dark and brooding. With his golden blonde hair and piercing blue eyes, he reminded her of a Norse conqueror.

Armoring herself to face that glimpse of flesh again, she turned with the books in hand, only to find he'd zipped up his jacket. Now the monitor leads protruded from the V. Had he seen where she'd been staring? Mortified that he might think she thought of him as a sexual object, she held out the casebooks to him.

Once again he surprised her by not taking them. "You can set them in one of the chairs." He raised his left arm and made the classic watch-checking gesture—but he wore no watch, only an IV taped to his hand.

"Damn." He scanned the room, looking for a clock.

"It's ten oh seven," Ciara said.

"Thanks. I need my watch. Would you look in my personal effects for it?"

Ciara stiffened to be treated as a servant when she was so much more than that. She laid the books on the bed next to him and then followed his orders.

But the tiny closet was empty. "There's nothing in here, Mr. Gannon."

"It must be in the ICU then. I'm trying to find a case on racketeering I vaguely remember. It would have been from about five years ago." He rubbed his right temple with two fingers and frowned.

The light went on in Ciara's mind. As ill as Bryce had been, it was natural for him to have difficulty with memory recall. The jogging suit and case files had masked his debilitation.

"I know the one you want," she said, especially since she'd seen which casebooks he'd requested. She picked up a book, perused the index and found the case. Then she handed the book to him.

Bryce took it, careful of his IV, and scanned the first page. "This is the one." Nodding, he continued to read.

Ciara warmed with pleasure, feeling stupidly pleased to aid him. She tried to squelch that feeling and remember why she was here.

"I can work from this," he said.

"On the Steele defense," she realized aloud. Disappointment warred with annoyance inside her.

He speared her with his icy stare. "Yes. I assume you know at least something about the case."

That was his cross-examination face. Did he suspect the reason she was here? Her heart skipped a beat in fear and then she scoffed at her paranoia. How could he?

"I know what everyone else who reads the newspaper knows. Adam Steele was arrested for racketeering and you're defending him. The case goes to federal court in less than two weeks. Or will you ask for a delay?" she tacked on, eyeing him where he lay.

"No delay." His answer was curt. He moved restlessly.

Ciara tried to bite back her concerns, but they tumbled out. "But you're in no condition—"

"I'll be well enough by then," he cut her off. His blue eyes were wintry.

Rebuked, Ciara met frost with the cool hauteur her mother had displayed as she ignored her husband's affairs. "One wonders if you're suicidal, why you didn't succumb to the ricin."

His eyes widened, and then narrowed. "One wonders if you wanted this job so badly, how you'd dare to speak to your employer that way."

Her gaze met his without flinching. "One wonders if you love your firm so much, why you'd risk it—and your life—for this case."

"If I fall in battle, you could win my firm. You're bold enough to do it."

Yes, she could picture him as a Roman Centurion, tall and proud. "I'm not arrogant enough to think I could replace you." Their banter thrilled her and made her feel more alive.

Bryce snorted. "You have arrogance in spades. It's aggression you lack."

His comment hurt more than it should have. She'd finished second in law school. She'd never been captain of her basketball team and her team had never won a championship. Yet her family thought her too aggressive, and not feminine enough, pursuing a man's profession and a man's sport.

How could she simultaneously be too aggressive and not aggressive enough?

Ciara felt her face stiffen. "What do you want me to do?"

Bryce's face wiped free of emotion. He was intuitive enough to sense her withdrawal. For several long moments he just stared at her. The only movement was the monitor readouts registering his life signs.

She didn't fidget under his regard, that stare that broke witnesses. She'd spent her adulthood fighting for her place in a man's world. She may have come in second, but she'd beaten the rest to be here.

Bryce breathed. Had she not been staring him down, she would have missed the infinitesimal wince of discomfort. She saw but gave no indication she'd seen. He was a proud man. She'd let him keep his pride.

"Research this case." He handed her the book. For a moment their hands brushed. A thrill ran through her and she jerked away. She could not feel anything for this man.

His face was impassive as ever. "See if there were any appeals or reversals. Find similar cases. Report your findings to me later." He waved her away and reached for his file. She wondered who'd brought it to him.

She couldn't spy on him from his office. She had to be in close proximity. "If you don't mind, I'll work here." As he opened his mouth to argue, she rushed on. "You may need something else and I'd rather be here when you do."

The heat in Bryce's eyes told her she'd said something wrong. When she played back the words in her mind, she read other meanings into them and blushed. She was no temptress, and it was well documented that Bryce preferred blondes. Just because he'd been several weeks without his beauty queen didn't mean he'd turn to *her* to assuage his needs.

Thank God Bryce didn't respond to her gaff. She retreated to the couch and sat where she had a good view of him. It would have been much easier to do the research with a table in front of her instead of holding the book on her knees, but this wasn't her reason for being here. Although she wouldn't shirk the work— she'd never done less than her best on anything.

As she wrote notes, so did he. More awkwardly, in fact, since he was lying in bed. She bit her tongue. His over-the-bed table was within reach. Why didn't he use it?

Bryce caught her staring. "What?"

"Do you need me to move the table?"

Again his eyes turned wintry. "No."

Proud man, she thought again.

"Miss Alafita, I don't want your pity."

"I don't pity you."

"Don't ever start."

They worked in mostly companionable silence for an hour. When he did speak to give her more ideas to research, his voice grew progressively more hoarse and breathy. She became alarmed.

When a knock sounded and a young woman in maroon scrubs appeared in the doorway, Bryce grimaced.

"Hi, Mr. Gannon. It's time for your breathing treatment." She was a short, perky, twenty-something brunette. She glanced at Ciara.

"Miss Alafita, I'll need you to leave the room for about twenty minutes. If you could track down my personal belongings during that time, I'd appreciate it." Bryce dismissed her.

Ciara hadn't gone through college and law school, passed the bar and worked her way to the AG's office to run personal errands for someone. She wasn't Bryce's wife or girlfriend either. She shoved her anger into that place inside her that smoldered, forced a smile, and went down to the nurse's station.

A frustrating forty-five minutes later she entered Bryce's room carrying two sealed biohazard bags at the end of her outstretched arm and gloved hand.

Bryce's eyes snapped with temper when he saw her and he opened his mouth. Whatever he'd planned to say died when he saw what she carried. His eyes widened.

She walked right up to the bed with her well-searched-for prizes. "Your personal effects."

Bryce didn't move to take them. "Are they . . . hazardous?"

"The hospital hazmat department thinks they're probably safe. Any ricin remaining on them is safe to handle if you wash your hands with soap immediately afterwards. And there's little chance of breathing in ricin, but in your case you might want to wear a mask. Their advice, not mine."

She smiled and continued. "They didn't want to destroy your Rolex watch because a jeweler should be able to clean it. The cell phone didn't appear to be affected, but just in case you might want it downloaded into a new phone. Your wallet and keys seemed unaffected as well, but you can't be too cautious. Oh, and you're to tell anyone handling the items that you were poisoned by airborne ricin. You wouldn't believe what I had to do to track these things down."

"I thought you said they were safe," he growled. His voice was less husky.

"They are, with provisos."

"You're wearing a glove," he accused.

"It's just precautionary. The bags didn't touch the ricin."

Since he didn't reach out to take them, Ciara laid them on his over-the-bed table. They sat there like a coiled rattlesnake. She pulled the glove off inside out, located the trash can and threw it away.

Bryce looked up from the bags to her. "I hate to ask what happened to my clothes."

"Incinerated with the other biohazardous material."

"My shoes too?"

"Yes. Expensive were they?" She knew they had to be.

"Hand-stitched Italian leather. I waited months for them."

She grimaced in sympathy. "I guess you should have said something in the ER." It gave her a perverse thrill to prod him.

"I was unconscious."

Oh.

Suddenly he reached for the phone and jabbed the buttons. "Get me Sharron." He waited, staring at the bags again. "Sharron, it's Bryce. Was the ricin cleaned from my office?"

He grimaced as he listened, caught Ciara watching him, and smoothed the expression from his face. He was really good at doing that. He must have had lots of practice.

"Thanks, Sharron." He hung up. "Everything paper had to be destroyed, but at least they let Sharron copy the plastic-covered documents so we didn't lose anything valuable. Just the originals. And the hazmat company was kinder than the hospital was."

"You're alive," she reminded him.

"There is that," he agreed. "And friends matter more than material things."

He looked away, so he missed her jerk of surprise. She hadn't expected him to say something like that, especially after his fuss over the expensive personal items. Bryce Gannon was enigmatic, like his courtroom face.

"Let's get back to work," he said.

Ciara checked on Bryce frequently at first during the next hour. His entire focus was on the case, frowning as he wrote pages of notes. Part of her admired his work ethic, but part of her cursed him for how he was expending his fragile energy. Was it that important to get one more bad guy off on some legal technicality or loophole? Or maybe Steele was the key to the lucrative mob business.

Maybe Bryce needed the money badly to maintain his expensive lifestyle. He was a very successful attorney, but some people lived far beyond their means. She made a mental note to tell the AG to look into Bryce's finances.

Her nose had begun to register food scents carried on the air conditioning when a movement caught her eye. A dark head looked around the opening door, spotted Bryce and pushed the door fully open.

Ciara recognized the couple from the news. Gabrielle Ziko's straight black hair and high cheekbones proclaimed her Native American heritage. The dark-haired, blue-eyed man at her back was her new husband, the infamous Christian Ziko, the only truly innocent man Gannon had defended in recent history.

Gabrielle carried a white bag from a Chinese restaurant. Christian kept his hand on her back. Two sets of blue eyes glanced curiously at Ciara, who remained seated, her pen poised above her legal pad, every sense alert. According to the newspapers, Gabrielle was a psychic, able to ferret out the truth, but she had to touch someone to do it. Ciara didn't know if she believed it or not.

Bryce watched them approach, his face expressionless.

But when Christian held out his hand, Bryce took it immediately.

"Roger and Paul were worried sick," Christian informed him. "I told them a cold snake like you was hard to kill."

Ciara stiffened, but a slight smile played at the corner of Bryce's mouth. "How long did you wait to tell them that?"

"Until you woke up."

Bryce nodded.

"I almost didn't recognize you in those clothes," Christian went on. He was teasing Bryce.

"I do have a life outside my office." Bryce's voice dripped irony. "Ask your brother."

"We didn't come to cross swords," Gabrielle interrupted, inserting herself between her husband and Bryce. "We brought you lunch."

"But you came for another reason, didn't you?" Bryce guessed.

Gabrielle glanced at Ciara. "Maybe. Who's your visitor?"

Bryce performed the introductions. By virtue of balancing the casebook and notebook on her knees, Ciara made herself unavailable to shake hands.

Now that Ciara had been identified, Gabrielle turned her attention back to Bryce. She lifted her chin. "With your permission?"

Ciara held her breath. Bryce hesitated, and then held out his hand to Gabrielle. She gripped it in both of hers. Christian's arm stole around her waist.

After a minute, Gabrielle gently pulled away. She looked right at Ciara and Ciara forgot to breathe. Her skin prickled. Was Gabrielle really a psychic? Had the other woman seen Ciara's involvement, and if so, how much had she seen?

Christian tucked Gabrielle tight against his side, nuzzling her temple, and their love for each other was nearly a palpable thing. It was a deep intimacy Ciara felt uncomfortable sharing. Her body heated in a flush.

"We didn't know you'd have a visitor," Gabrielle apologized. "I'm sorry, Miss Alafita, but we didn't bring you anything to eat."

Ciara rose, desperate to escape, and stuffed her tablet in her briefcase. "That's all right. I need to get some more casebooks from the office. Bryce, do you need anything?" Her voice was too high and fast, her movements too rushed.

Bryce frowned, but handed her a sheet of paper. She took it, careful not to touch him.

"I'll be back in a few hours." She forced a smile for the Zikos. "It was nice meeting you."

Then she fled down the hall to the elevator. With a bit of luck the car came right away and no one joined her inside. She leaned against the cool metal wall, taking long, deep breaths, as she tried to calm her thundering heart. For a few moments when the newlyweds clasped one another, she'd felt a longing so strong for a love like theirs that her chest had tightened and her eyes had pricked with tears.

She'd resigned herself that she'd never marry. Her parent's example had destroyed any illusions she might have had about happily ever after. Her father lived with his bimbo mistress and their love child, even though he was still married to her mother. Her mother lived with her daughter now, after putting up with her husband's infidelities their entire marriage because she thought that's how Latin males acted. She'd still be living with him if his mistress hadn't gotten pregnant. Apparently that made Ciara's mother unable to turn a blind eye to his philandering ways.

No, Ciara had no illusions about marriage. But for an instant watching the Zikos, she'd wanted to believe.

CHAPTER 4

"Who is she really, Bryce?" Gabrielle asked after Ciara fled the room.

Bryce turned from staring at the empty doorway, filing away the mystery of Ciara's hasty retreat to examine at another time.

"I only know what she and her boss told me. I don't know anything for sure. What did you see?"

"It was a precognitive vision, Bryce. You know they're rare for me. You were angry. She said you owed her an apology. But you felt betrayed. You said, 'I believe it's the other way around. Who spied on whom? Who lied to whom?' I wish I could have touched her and found out how she betrays you so we could prevent it."

Bryce knew already. He was wary of her and he knew better than to trust her. "You don't have to worry about me."

"Yes, we do," Christian said. "If Gabrielle says Miss Alafita will betray you, you need to be careful."

"I am being careful." Keep your enemies closer.

Christian and Gabrielle looked at one another, and she shrugged.

"I hope you like Chinese." Christian took the bag from his wife's hand.

Bryce went with the change in topic and mood. "Of course. The hospital has been feeding me only soft foods. I don't know what they're afraid of."

"They probably heard your reputation." Christian reached for the rolling table where the biohazard bags still rested and jerked to a halt. "What's that?"

Bryce told them as he took courage and the bags in both hands and moved them. The ricin couldn't get out of the bags, couldn't hurt him further.

The food was delicious, spicy after the bland hospital diet. The Zikos stood to eat—in deference to him—and fed one another out of their Styrofoam containers. When they leaned in for a quick kiss, Bryce busied himself with his own food.

They were newlyweds, still in the throes of newly discovered sexual desire and the first blush of love. Bryce wondered if they'd still be in love like this in five or ten years. He hoped so, but he had no example of a strong, lasting marriage based on love to compare them to. His parents hadn't been by the time Bryce was born, if they'd ever been. Roger had lost interest in both his wives, and so had Paul, although he at least seemed to regret the loss.

Bryce had experienced desire but not love. He'd thought because of his parents' example he never would. He'd been a groomsman for Roger and Paul, but seemed immune to marriage. So when he'd reached thirty-nine without falling in love he'd coldly considered a marriage to Monique Dennison.

But after he'd seen Christian with Gabrielle, what Bryce shared with Monique hadn't been enough. He didn't know what he wanted. The Zikos' almost desperate passion and constant touching didn't tempt him. But the way they looked at one another . . . he wanted a woman to look at him like that.

Seeing them together, sharing something he'd never experienced firsthand and barely understood, made him ache. Yet it warmed a place inside him, a place without a name.

"Bryce, don't you like your food?" Gabrielle asked.

"Sorry. I was thinking about my case."

"You shouldn't be working so soon," Christian said.

"You, of all people, should understand why I'm working," Bryce responded. "Finishing this case is as important to me as resurrecting your business is to you."

"But you're doing this by yourself. I had Gabrielle and Roger. And Gabrielle was at home with me."

"Roger, Paul and Sean are checking on me. And my housekeeper takes care of me at home."

The couple shared a look, the universal one of the newly married who thought theirs was the better state.

"That's not the same thing," Gabrielle denied.

Bryce had recently begun to appreciate the difference. If only he could find a woman who could be his equal, who could arouse emotion in him as well as lust. His mind provided an image of Ciara Alafita—beautiful, poised, intelligent, and able to carry her weight in an argument with him. If Ciara wasn't a spy for Adam Steele …

"Speaking of your business, how's it going?" Bryce asked to change the subject. Besides, he really wanted to know. It was time he paid more attention to his friends.

Funny, he'd been aware of Christian through his older brother Paul since Christian was ten years old, but due to the decade age difference between them, he and Christian hadn't been friends. But something had changed recently and now Christian—and Gabrielle—had become people he could count on.

Bryce toyed with the idea of talking to Christian about the lung damage. Christian took medicine every day for bipolar disorder, so he'd be able to empathize on a more personal level. But Bryce's diagnosis was too new to discuss with anyone but Sean. And even with Sean, Bryce hadn't let his feelings loose. He was afraid what would happen if he did.

That evening, when Paul Ziko arrived, Bryce insisted on having a shower. He'd lain in bed all day like a good boy, conserving his strength while he shared his room with a beautiful woman. He considered the shower part of his armoring. It took Paul, a nurse, and an orderly to prep him and get the job done. Being a former college athlete and now belonging to a gym, he had little modesty in the dressing room or shower. But he didn't care to repeat this experience. He demanded the removal of the IV. He swore he'd take the damn pills rather than be tied to that pole one more day.

He watched part of the Detroit Tigers baseball game with Paul. His friend seemed sunk in his own sad thoughts, but Bryce didn't know what to say to Paul. He'd had it all—a loving wife, two wonderful kids, and a house in the suburbs—and he'd thrown it all away to have an affair. Bryce had thought Paul the solid one; after all, he'd raised Christian after their parents died. But Paul went astray somehow—like they all had. Now Paul couldn't find his way back. Bryce hoped being with a friend helped.

Two days later, when Bryce had adjusted to his inhalers, he demanded to go home.

• • •

Ciara rang the doorbell a second time. Bryce was supposed to be expecting her. This sprawling gray brick house in Grosse Pointe Woods, a wealthy Detroit suburb, must have cost him a fortune. She'd expected Bryce to own a condo—without maintenance or upkeep.

Bryce had been poisoned less than a week ago. He'd gone home from the hospital a lot sooner than she'd believed possible. It was that iron will of his. She'd seen it from the very first day she'd worked with him. He pushed himself with a determination she would have admired if he'd been doing it for some reason other than the Steele case.

The door jerked open and there stood the Bryce Gannon from the TV footage—blonde hair meticulously combed off a wide forehead and held in place by styling product that leached the warm gold from his hair. He wore a blinding white, starched shirt. She'd never seen him in any other color. He wore navy trousers and a green tie with navy and white rectangles. She'd never seen him in a plain tie either. His clothes looked tailor-made and fit him well, displaying how in shape his body was.

It was a shock to see him this way after the way he'd looked in the hospital. He felt like a stranger now.

"Are you coming in or are you going to gawk at me all day? You've seen me before." Bryce's mouth twisted in a wry almost-smile.

Ciara jerked her chin up and stepped over the threshold. As he closed the door, she explained, "I hadn't expected to see you in a suit. It's Sunday." She was also surprised to see him on his feet. He'd remained in bed while in the hospital. Obviously there'd been a vast improvement since she'd left him Friday afternoon.

Standing beside him made her body quiver with awareness. He seemed so much more masculine and dominant now. She smelled a hint of aftershave, very light and undoubtedly expensive.

"I'm dressed for work," he said.

"Are you going to the office?" If so, why hadn't he asked her to meet him there, in a less intimate setting?

His hesitation was infinitesimal. "Not today."

Bryce turned and led the way down a main hall with rooms branching off it. She dragged her eyes away from how the navy trousers molded his firm hips and buttocks to her surroundings. The woodwork had expensive wainscoting and crown molding. He entered a room on the left, which turned out to be a spacious study big enough for a black leather couch, lots of bookshelves, and a large mahogany desk.

Ciara examined the books. They were older casebooks. The ones in his office were newer.

As he stopped beside his desk, he noticed where she was looking. "My first reference books."

She'd never owned casebooks. He owned two sets.

"I had the discovery files delivered here." He indicated a line of file boxes on the thick cream carpet. "I want to go through every bit of evidence the prosecutor has and find rebuttals."

His office manager had to be at his beck and call twenty-four seven since she'd called Ciara late yesterday to ask her to work with Bryce at his home today. Then Sharron must have arranged delivery of the files.

Ciara took her notepad from her briefcase and sat down on the couch, smoothing her skirt. She was lucky only her work clothes were clean, so she'd worn them. She would have felt at a disadvantage dressed in casual clothes while Bryce wore a suit. And she didn't want that. She pulled the closest box to her.

Bryce picked up the box furthest from her and carried it to his desk. The loud thump it made when it hit the desk startled her into glancing up. He was grimacing and his left arm hugged his chest.

"Don't hurt yourself so you have to go back to the hospital."

Bryce glared at her but said nothing. She wondered if he could talk at that moment. He grabbed papers from the box and settled in his chair with them.

After a while he spoke. "You'll need to interview this witness, Hasan. I think we can dispute his testimony's relevance to the case against the client."

"All right. When?"

"Call him and see if you can interview him today. He's probably at home." Bryce held out the file folder towards her.

He was an authoritative man who expected instant compliance. She rose and took the file from him, then gestured to the phone on his desk.

"Do you mind if I call from here?"

Bryce vacated his seat and rifled through the box again. She sat in the soft black leather chair, still warm with his body heat. A frisson of unwanted awareness zinged through her.

As she dialed the phone, she scanned his desk. There was only one framed photo. In it Bryce stood with three other men—she identified Roger Barrett and Paul Ziko—in front of a lake. All wore casual clothes and looked happy and relaxed. The photo had to be ten years old. Bryce's blonde hair—free of styling gel—was a warm gold.

He showed steadfast loyalty to his male friends, yet there was no record he'd ever been engaged or married. Her father had taught her that men didn't practice fidelity. Bryce couldn't even commit to one woman.

Mr. Hasan could see her, so she made an appointment for within the hour. She turned to find Bryce listening beside her. Her body heated with his proximity. Her heartbeat sped up. Her breathing became shallow and then stopped altogether as he leaned towards her.

He pulled open the side drawer and handed her a small tape recorder. "Record the interview."

Ciara's breath whooshed out. She was being stupid. She oriented her thoughts to reality—she was Bryce's researcher, not his love interest. Audiotapes were standard procedure with some lawyers.

"You could come with me."

Bryce shook his head. "I've got too much work to do."

• • •

Sunday morning Detroit traffic was light. Mr. Hasan was frightened by her questions, as he should be. Bryce intended to get Adam Steele off so he could continue his reign of terror against business owners like Hasan. She had difficulty not siding with him openly and ground her teeth in frustration against her situation. Finding out the truth about Bryce was protecting the public. But helping Bryce defend a lawbreaker went against all her principals.

She said as much to the AG on the drive back to Bryce's house.

"I'm sorry you have to work on the case, Ciara. I hadn't expected that," Attorney General Baisden said. "Although it's an unlooked-for opportunity to see how corrupt the bastard really is. I'm amazed he's working already. He was just discharged yesterday."

"He's worked from his hospital bed the last few days."

"He must really want to get Steele acquitted and quickly."

"He's driven, but I'm not sure yet what's driving him. I can't read him."

"That could be because he's been ill."

"No, I think it's more than that." She'd reached the freeway on-ramp, so she had to end the call too soon. "Before I forget, he's got expensive tastes and he lives in an expensive house in Grosse Pointe Woods. I can't tell if he lives beyond his means or not."

"I'll check on his finances."

"I have to go."

Although she was sent to spy, she felt a traitor for baring Bryce's secrets. If only she'd kept tighter control of her feelings, she wouldn't be in this situation. She could learn something from Bryce's example.

When she returned to his home, Ciara parked deeper in Bryce's driveway and entered through the back door as he'd instructed. She noted with delighted surprise the basketball hoop set into the concrete in the secluded niche that fronted the garage.

She found Bryce in his office where she'd left him, surrounded by files and papers.

"Did you get what we need?" he asked.

"Yes. There's no direct tie to the client."

"That may be enough." He nodded and went back to his files.

Ciara's conscience twinged that what she'd done would aid Steele's defense and not the prosecution's case against him. It didn't help knowing Bryce would have noticed the discrepancy, would have interviewed the witness himself and gotten the damning testimony. She felt that if Steele got away it would be her fault.

After several hours of reading, her eyes began to cross and her back and shoulders ached from how she was sitting on the couch. A glance at her watch showed it was nearly lunchtime. The basketball hoop called her name. She could flex her muscles a little before lunch.

As she rose, Bryce's gaze crossed hers. "I need to stretch my legs and get some fresh air." She snagged her car keys from her purse.

The temperature was already mid-eighties, but for once the humidity was low. She'd probably sweat in her business attire, but her clothes wouldn't stick to her.

In moments she'd removed her slings and replaced them with her court shoes. She scooped her basketball from her trunk. She carried shorts and a tank top with her, too, but she didn't intend for an all-out game of hoops, just a little limbering up.

It took a few minutes to feel comfortable shooting hoops in her A-line skirt, but the long kick pleat in the back made it easier. Soon she lost herself in her one-on-one against the hoop.

As she sank another basket, she reflected that her parents hadn't understood how this activity both challenged and soothed her. It was a boy's sport, they'd insisted, not fit for a girl. But she loved it.

She missed a couple of shots, felt a little rusty and attempted that same shot over and over until her movements were smooth again and she sank three in a row.

The sound of clapping snapped her head around. Bryce stood on the concrete back steps leaning against the black wrought iron railing watching her.

Ciara's cheeks burned. He'd caught her not only goofing off on his company time, but being a jock.

"You're good," he said.

His praise made her heartbeat flutter. She twirled the basketball on her finger. "I played in college."

"Four years?"

"Yes. Basketball scholarship. Then I played pick-up games in law school. I worked out with the team when I could."

"Why didn't you go pro?"

"I wasn't that good." She shrugged as though it meant nothing. In fact, she would have been thrilled to be asked to play in the WNBA. But no team had courted her.

Bryce came slowly down the cement steps. He held out his hands for the ball and she tossed it to him. He walked to the foul line, studied the hoop, and made his shot. It missed.

"I haven't played in a while," he explained.

Ciara retrieved the ball. "I wish we could play a little one-on-one."

"Hmm, sounds delightful," he fairly purred.

Realizing what spin he'd put on the words, Ciara blushed. She couldn't believe how much that thought tantalized her. She dragged her mind back to the here and now.

"When you feel better, we can play and I'll spot you points."

"Ow. You're hell on a man's ego." His voice held a sharp edge.

Ciara stiffened at his tone and his words. "I can't be less than I am." It came out sounding stuffy because she was strangling her anger.

"No, I can see that. Well I can't either. Let's try a little one-one-one anyway." Bryce looked from his shoes to her court shoes. "Another disadvantage."

"Bryce, you're in no condition to play."

"Then you have nothing to be afraid of. Give me the ball." His autocratic demand matched his glacial glare.

"Here." She bounced the ball to him, purposely not thrusting it directly at him.

He held it in front of him in both hands, his legs flexed at the knee. "Well, what are you waiting for?"

"Bryce, you just got out of the hospital. This is stupid. You don't have to prove anything to me."

"You really don't think much of me at the moment, do you, Miss Alafita?"

Ciara sighed and took up guard position in front of him. She'd hurt his ego and now he had to beat his chest to prove he was a real man. This was a major mistake.

He tried to feint right around her, but she blocked him. She'd shut him down right here and now. But the impact of his hard, warm body sent sensual shocks through her. Her heart pounded like a trapped thing.

Bryce bounced the ball and tried the other direction. She moved in front of him with arms raised, not really trying, just standing in his way. She didn't know if she wanted him to brush against her again or not.

He spun the other way and ducked under her arms. She turned with him and slid around in front of him as he went for a lay-up. She jumped with him to block the shot. His chest rubbed against her breasts, which tightened at the contact.

Ciara heard the clunk of the ball hitting the rim. All her molecules tried to reorient themselves to the court when what they wanted was to rub against him over and over, like a cat. With an effort she jerked her hormones to heel.

She turned in time to catch the ball. Then it was her turn at offense. She didn't have a good set-up from where she stood, so she tried to get around Bryce. But he moved with her. His face, although flushed, was a deadly mask of competitive intensity.

Ciara feinted and twisted, but Bryce always seemed to be there. Then she slipped past him and went for the picture perfect lay-up. The ball barely kissed the rim as it fell through the hoop.

Yes. She spun to smile at Bryce, but her smile died. He was bent over, hands on knees, gasping for breath. She rushed to his side, berating herself for a fool for letting him push her into playing. He wasn't up to much physical exertion yet. She was as big an idiot as he was.

"Bryce, where's your oxygen?" Panic made her heart trip like she was playing all out basketball.

He waved her away, and then patted his chest. His breath whistled in and out in a terrifying sound. Then there was a round disk in his hand, which he put to his mouth and inhaled.

An inhaler. She recognized it from TV commercials. Relief nearly buckled her knees. He took a second drag and the whistling stopped. Slowly his breathing eased and he straightened. Sweat beaded his flushed face as he took in great gulps of air.

"Sit down, Bryce."

Ciara tried to take his arm, but he shrugged her off. After a moment, however, he moved to the steps and sat down.

His face could have been carved from stone. Worse than his courtroom face, this expression reminded her of iron control crushing something. She hovered by him, uncertain what to do. Her tight muscles screamed at her to do something. He didn't look at her.

"Get your things and get out." His voice was weak and hoarse, and all the more terrible for it.

"I think you need somebody with you."

His glare could have seared a hole through her. "Get out or you're fired."

Belatedly she realized he thought she pitied him. It wasn't pity but fear. She scrambled to reassure him. "Bryce, your debilitation is only temporary."

"You're fired." His words were cold and lethal.

Oh, God, she had to finish this assignment. She lifted her chin. Her mother had taught her determination in the face of all odds. "I don't think so." She made a point of looking at her watch. "I'm on my lunch hour. I haven't done anything on this court you could fire me for. My playing ball hasn't affected my work performance, and you told me you were satisfied with that. If anyone's behavior were questionable, it would be yours, since you made a pass at me. Any court in Detroit would award me a wrongful termination suit. And I don't think you want that, Mr. Gannon.

"No, I believe I'll stay and finish what we started."

Bryce still glared, but that horrible stoniness had left his face. "Were you this much trouble to your last employer?" His voice was low but succinct.

"I'm not trouble. You're just not used to having an equal on your team. I'm the only other full-fledged lawyer in your office." She suddenly realized how odd that was for a lawyer as successful as he was. But before she could wonder what it meant, Bryce pulled himself upright.

Ciara was so relieved that he wasn't firing her, she blurted, "Would you like me to pick up some lunch?"

He eyed her, and then the corner of his mouth twitched. "I wouldn't condescend to ask or order a practicing attorney to do such a menial task."

She blinked. He'd made a joke. "We have to eat."

"My housekeeper put something in the fridge."

Housekeeper. Another example of his affluence. "I have to put my ball in the trunk. I'll be there in a minute."

Ciara turned so she wouldn't watch Bryce climb the stairs. She collected her ball and strode out of sight to her car. There she leaned against the opened trunk and took in great gulps of air.

She would never have spoken that way to Bryce if this had been a real job. She'd spoken as though she had balls. Her mother would be mortified. A delicate shudder ran through Ciara. She wasn't mortified at all. In fact, she felt rejuvenated. She'd stood toe to toe with Bryce Gannon as an equal and won. When had he gone from fool to equal?

CHAPTER 5

Ciara had looked hot playing basketball in that tight skirt. Bryce shook his head to dispel the image, but it wouldn't go away. She was cool and reserved in that skirt and knit top, all business with her hair upswept. But get her on a basketball court and that long body moved with a fluidity that set his blood on fire.

And the joy on her face. She hadn't even been aware he was watching she'd been so wrapped up in something she clearly loved. Yet she'd given it up to practice law. Why? And then she'd allegedly given up the AG's office for her family. Her behavior didn't make sense. What part did Adam Steele play in her illogical decisions?

Then, to top it all off, she'd talked back to him, her employer, risking the job that allowed her to live close to her family. Wasn't she afraid of Steele's wrath if she lost this job? But Bryce couldn't concentrate on her inconsistencies. All he could think about was the way her body had felt against his—warm and toned, her nipples peaked with the same desire he felt. His sexual engine had gone from off to turbocharged in seconds.

He wanted her. But she was right about one thing—she worked for him and passes from a superior to an employee were sexual harassment.

If they were unwanted.

Ciara hadn't seemed repulsed by him. Would she welcome his attention? Could he risk it knowing whom she spied for? Would she report his behavior to Steele? Or, unpalatable thought, would her boss encourage her to bed Bryce to keep him happy? His muscles tightened in protest. Well thank God he wasn't up for anything sexual, so the point was moot.

Bryce rooted in the refrigerator for the chicken salad plates Mrs. McCleary had made while Ciara interviewed Hasan and placed them on the island counter. He had just grabbed a couple of bottled waters when Ciara entered the kitchen. His body reacted immediately to the sight of her flushed cheeks and lithe body. His pulse sped up, his groin tightened, and he felt hyper alert to her presence. He turned back to the cupboards to hide his reaction while he dug forks out of the silverware drawer.

"That looks good," Ciara said.

He turned back to find her on the other side of the island. "Mrs. McCleary swears by the Food Network."

Ciara eyed the plates. "Did she have to make a special trip over for this?"

"She comes in almost every day to cook and clean." Bryce motioned for Ciara to take her plate and follow him to the table by the window. "She went out to get groceries. She'll be back this afternoon."

"I guess she didn't expect you out of the hospital so soon. I can't imagine hearing something terrible about my employer on the news."

"She didn't hear it there first. Paul or Sean, or maybe Roger, called her."

When Ciara frowned at him, he clarified, "My friends. They have limited power of attorney for me in case I'm incapacitated."

"That came in handy. But why them and not your family?"

"I don't have any family."

When Ciara's face softened into an expression resembling pity and she opened her mouth to make a comment, Bryce froze her into silence with a look. He sure as hell didn't miss his parents.

Ciara ate for a few moments before asking, "How long has Mrs. McCleary been with you?"

Bryce appreciated the change of topic. "Five years." Since his caseload had grown and he'd realized he'd probably never fall in love and find a wife to take care of him.

"I guess as successful as you've become, you need a housekeeper."

Bryce laid down his fork. "Is that what you think of my life?"

Ciara gestured around her. "This house, the housekeeper, your Rolex—they're status symbols."

"You don't know anything about me." He jabbed a chunk of pineapple with his fork. He wasn't ostentatious or flashy. He didn't flaunt his earnings. He liked quality goods that lasted and clothes that fit well.

"Then tell me about Bryce Gannon."

"I thought you researched me when you were looking for a job."

Ciara flushed. "I didn't learn things like that you had a housekeeper."

"Lots of people who work for a living pay someone to clean. Mine cooks too and runs errands. I work a lot of hours. It's how I'm successful." He couldn't help his curiosity about her, and hoped he could also trick her into showing her hand. "Don't you hire it done?"

"The hotel maid service does everything at the moment."

He pounced. "Hotel?"

"Well I intended to find an apartment, but your office manager offered me the position right away. So I'm in an extended stay hotel. Now I can take my time finding the right place to live."

How convenient. She didn't really move here. The doorbell interrupted his planned cross-examination.

"Excuse me."

Bryce checked the front door's peephole and sighed. He opened the door to his former girlfriend and lover.

"Hello, Monique. This is a surprise."

She looked stunning in her chic casual summer outfit, her hair and make-up as perfect as ever.

She leaned forward and kissed him on the cheek. "I just got back into town and heard about the bomb. I'd planned to visit you in the hospital today. I couldn't believe it when they said you'd been released." Her blue eyes looked him up and down in clear disbelief.

"I'm fine. All I need is some rest."

One perfectly manicured hand indicated his suit. "Dressed for the office?"

"I have a big case to prepare for, Monique."

"Aren't you going to invite me in?"

Bryce had dated this woman and slept with her, but now he felt nothing for her. He'd felt more passion playing one-on-one with Ciara.

"Bryce?" Speaking of the devil, here was Ciara now.

• • •

Ciara recognized the former beauty queen immediately. Figure of a pin-up, face of a model, legs men chased after, perfect blonde hair. She had everything men thought Ciara lacked. Next to the former Miss Michigan, Ciara felt less feminine.

Monique Dennison stood very close to Bryce, possessively close. Her blue eyes widened and then narrowed at the sight of Ciara.

"I'm sorry, Bryce," she said. "I didn't realize you had company." Was that hurt in her voice?

"Hello Miss Dennison. I recognize you from your photo." The one with Bryce Ciara had seen during her research.

Ciara got the impression from the way Monique had been looking at Bryce that she might be having second thoughts about their breakup.

"Monique, this is Ciara Alafita, my new legal assistant." Bryce's voice sounded stiff. Did he wish Ciara hadn't interrupted?

"Bryce and I were having lunch," Ciara explained with extreme politeness. "Would you like to join us?" Already she felt like a fifth wheel.

Monique looked from Ciara to Bryce. "No, thank you. I can see I'm interrupting. Bryce, I brought some of the things you left at my condo." She waved at a box on the porch behind her.

"I appreciate that, Monique."

"I didn't know if you needed anything. Even though we're not together anymore, I know you better than anyone. I thought you might be more comfortable with me helping you recuperate. But I see you don't need help." Monique sounded like she was trying to hide her upset.

"Now that I know you're all right, I won't keep you from your lunch." She turned and walked with beauty queen grace down the steps to her car.

Bryce tugged the box inside and closed the door.

Ciara debated with herself for a moment, and then said, "I think she wants you back."

He gave her a sharp look. "You're mistaken."

Ciara narrowed her eyes at him. It was possible the blonde got tired of Bryce's coldness, but Ciara would swear the former Miss Michigan still wanted him. Had Bryce had a secret affair Monique couldn't accept, so she'd walked away? But like Ciara's mother, she'd decided to forgive Bryce's indiscretion and take him back? Did she think Ciara was the other woman? Ciara shuddered at the thought.

"You two look like the perfect couple," she said. Like Barbie and Ken.

"There's more to a relationship than looks."

Ciara's mouth dropped open in surprise. That was like saying blonde hair and big boobs weren't enough. No man in her experience said that.

Yet Bryce had let a woman men would break their wedding vows over walk away, and for what? Not another blonde, not even for another woman, or a man for that matter. He'd given up the American male's perfect dream girl to be alone as far as Ciara could tell.

Why, why, why? She had questions but no answers. Maybe she should concentrate on his professional life instead.

But later that afternoon, Bryce threw her another curve ball.

"Would you drive me to my office so I can get my car?"

Ciara nearly dropped the file she was reading. Her heart skipped a beat. "You're in no condition to drive."

At Bryce's glacial glare, she could have bitten her tongue.

"Will you drive me or should I call a cab?"

"Bryce, be reasonable. This is your first full day home. Why do you need your car anyway?"

"So I can go to the carry-out for cigarettes if I run out," he stated in a voice deadly serious.

Her mind's gears jammed. Had he made a joke . . . or a point? Giving him his car would be akin to giving a child a loaded gun. But if she didn't drive him to his office, she was sure he'd take a taxi. And either way, he'd be driving back here alone.

"I'll call a cab," she relented. When Bryce glared at her she explained, "I'm riding back here with you."

He looked mulish. "That's not necessary."

"I'm sorry you feel that way, but I can't in good conscience allow you to drive alone. What if you tire? What if you need to use your inhaler? I'm only being prudent."

"I don't need a nursemaid. I've driven since I was sixteen."

"But you've never had a near-fatal injury before, have you?"

Ciara suffered his courtroom glare, the one that broke witnesses. She raised her chin. *Bring it on.*

The moment elongated, but if Bryce thought she'd be the one to back down, he knew nothing about her. She'd fought harder than this against her mother and won, and for much higher stakes.

Bryce nodded, just once and only a slight movement. A little thrill ran through her that she hid by reaching for the phone.

The cab sped along the freeway toward Bryce's office in Sterling Heights. Traffic was congested and Ciara remembered the Tigers had an afternoon home game today. She chewed on her lower lip. What if Bryce's reaction time was off? Detroit's expressways were no place for an impaired driver. Was she literally putting her life on the line by riding with him?

The cab pulled up to his office building on 15 Mile and they exited. Bryce looked up at the modern multi-story building, his face impassive. He hadn't brought his briefcase with him, but she thought he might be considering going inside.

Instead, he turned and entered the underground parking garage. He scanned the lot and strode towards the first row of cars. He pointed his key fob at the row where a silver Mercedes sedan chirped and the lights blinked.

The E class was an older model, but still more car than many people could afford. Bryce opened the driver's side, a look of challenge and satisfaction on his face. Ciara sighed and slid in on the passenger's side. She turned towards Bryce so she could watch him for signs of strain.

The first thing she noticed was the car was a stick shift. Strange, she'd thought a luxury automobile would be automatic. Bryce grimaced as he worked the gearshift into neutral. The powerful engine roared to life and again Bryce used the shifter to reverse. His hands touched the controls with familiarity and ease. Only his set face showed the strain it was to drive a stick. He backed the car and spun the wheel to turn towards the exit.

By the time they reached it, sweat beaded Bryce's forehead. But his jaw was hard as granite. Grim determination described it best. Ciara held on as he accelerated towards the freeway, moving smoothly through the gears. His hands held the wheel tight. He didn't speed or change lanes to move around slower cars. Still, she was afraid to distract him from his driving.

But as they reached the freeway and merged into traffic, the speed of the powerful car evened out and Bryce relaxed. Well, as much as she thought he ever relaxed. The muscles in his jaw unclenched and his grip on the wheel eased.

In the driver's seat again, Ciara thought, and then realized the truth of that statement. Since the hospital Bryce had been pushing the limits others set for his recovery. *He* wanted to be in charge of his life. This car was a symbol for him. He controlled the gear changes. He decided direction. He went where he chose, when he chose. He had power over a more powerful object, and it was active control, not passive.

Maybe this facet of his personality had led to the breakup with Miss Michigan. A woman didn't win that crown by being passive. Maybe the blonde didn't always want to be in the passenger seat in the relationship—or in bed. Did Bryce dominate like this in bed?

A shivery feeling darted through her lower abdomen. It'd be interesting to test that theory.

When Bryce reached his house he pulled all the way to the back near the basketball court. Instead of putting the car in the garage, he turned off the engine.

"Are you going out again?" Ciara asked in alarm.

Bryce glanced at her. "I'm leaving my options open."

He had his courtroom face on, so she couldn't tell if he meant the remark or not. She wouldn't put it past him, just to prove he could.

The next morning he did just that. "I'm going to the office," Bryce told Ciara when she walked in his back door. "I need you to re-interview these witnesses for me." He held out a handwritten list.

"Bryce, you're supposed to be recuperating. You can't go to the office."

"The matter's not open for discussion," he said with cold disdain, and then grabbed her hand and tucked the list in it.

Ciara tried arguing some sense into him. "Is winning this case so important you'd risk your health for it?"

"Hell yes it is." He pointed his key fob at the kitchen window towards where his car was parked.

"Bryce—" Ciara began to protest.

The explosion shattered the kitchen windows and knocked Ciara and Bryce off their feet.

CHAPTER 6

"Omigod. That was a bomb," Ciara choked, her voice unsteady. She lay on her side, her back pressed to Bryce's chest. He'd grabbed her as they fell to soften the blow.

Bryce felt just as shaken and a little winded by the fall. His heartbeat raced with fight or flight, and felt like it was lodged in his throat. He had to get up. He couldn't lie here, as nice as it felt to be cuddled against Ciara's warm body. He rolled over, placing a hand on the floor, and a shard of glass stabbed his palm. Glass sparkled on the kitchen floor around them. He lifted his hand to see blood welling in the cut.

"We've got to call the police." Ciara made movements to rise.

"Be careful. There's glass everywhere."

"Ow. Yeah, I see that." She reached for her purse and dragged it to her. Glass tinkled as it moved. Several cars' alarms wailed nearby. As she found her cell phone, Bryce gripped the counter edge to pull himself up.

"Stay down," Ciara hissed. "You don't know who's out there."

"Bombers don't hang around to shoot you if they miss," Bryce said, his voice dripping disdain, although his belly shook with nerves. He didn't really know anything about what bombers did. He gained his feet, but his legs were shaky.

Ciara had reached the 911 operator and reported Bryce's address as she pushed herself to her feet.

Bryce looked out the almost glassless windows. Black smoke roiled from where he'd parked his car yesterday afternoon. Chunks of metal littered the basketball court.

"Tell them to send the fire department," he managed, although it was more of a croak. He needed to go outside to make sure the house wasn't on fire, but he felt frozen to the spot. Someone had tried to kill him—again.

He could feel his chest tighten and the drag on his lungs as he breathed. *Dammit, not now.* He forced his feet to move toward the back door, crunching through the broken glass.

"Bryce, don't go out there. Wait for the police."

The police hadn't caught the letter bomber. Now that person had graduated to real bombs. Damn Steele and his organization of greedy, power hungry bastards, playing with his life as though it were meaningless. Anger sped his pace. He yanked open the door and stepped outside. A few neighborhood dogs barked and in the distance a siren wailed. In this affluent suburb, he was sure it was the 911 response.

Bryce descended the steps and stalked across the basketball court. Halfway there he came to a dead stop.

His car was engulfed in flames. Black smoke rose into the morning sky. The hood was up in the air, the passenger door askew on its hinges. One of the hubcaps lay tilted at his feet. His knees nearly buckled. If he hadn't used the remote car starter …

He'd be dead.

He staggered the few feet to the side of the house and leaned against the brick. The smoke seared his already burning lungs, making him cough. He grabbed his inhaler and filled his lungs with the hated steroids. It fueled his anger that the medicine eased his breathing.

Luckily the car was far enough from the house that the flames couldn't reach. Twice now a fluke had saved him—a phone call had made him look away when the letter bomb exploded, and now this. He'd only had the remote car starter installed a month ago in preparation for the hot Detroit summer and long cold winter with a major trial beginning. But he didn't always use it.

Like yesterday, after the car had sat unused for nearly a week, he'd started it manually.

He'd been strangely lucky in his life. Even in the instance with the near-fatal hazing, he'd met Paul Ziko a short while beforehand, and it was Paul who'd recognized the danger and led his other friends to the rescue.

And then an uglier thought intruded. Ciara had just arrived. Could she have planted the bomb? *Don't be stupid*, he chided himself. He assumed it took longer than the minute from the time he'd heard her car pull into the driveway until she had walked in the back door.

But the ugly thoughts wouldn't stop. She was working for Steele. Maybe she also reported to Steele's competition. Maybe she'd told them he'd retrieved his car. No, that didn't make sense. Why not just bomb his house?

Without his willing it, his hand jerked back from the wall he leaned against. How hard would it be to kill him in a brick house? A lot harder than killing him in his car. At least by bombing the car, they'd be sure he was dead.

They'd failed with the ricin. This time they'd wanted to make sure.

"Bryce?"

He stiffened. They had a spy in his life, in his home. Who would suspect a beautiful woman? Who but him?

"Bryce, are you all right?" Ciara touched his arm and he had difficulty not jerking away from her.

"I liked that car." It was the safest thing he could say to throw her off the scent.

Even if she wasn't a double agent for Steele's adversary, if she reported to anyone but Steele she could still be a dupe. She could be reporting what she thought were innocuous things, but were in fact things that could get him killed. While keeping him locked in Steele's trap, she left him vulnerable to hunters and other predators.

God, he hated this. He couldn't chuck it all and walk away. His only friends were here and probably as vulnerable as he was. They could be targeted to make him come to heel. If he didn't care, he could walk away from Steele's trap. But he did care. He knew of only one way to keep him and his friends safe—that was to get Steele locked away for life.

But trying to do that while pretending to get Steele acquitted—without arousing Ciara's suspicions—would be a dangerous and difficult undertaking.

"Bryce, it's okay to be rattled by this. You could have been in the car."

"Yeah. Well I wasn't. Your car's hood is dented, by the way."

Her head snapped around and she swore.

"You probably want to move it before the fire department gets here," Bryce added.

Ciara frowned at him, and then whirled and headed back to the house. Her concern seemed so real. It was something he wanted badly. He had to remember she was playing a part. She was his jailor. Even if she was only working for Steele and not for the people who wanted him dead, she was paid to lie to him. He couldn't count on her for anything in the long run but deception and betrayal.

Bryce watched the fire department douse the flames. He suffered the Grosse Pointe Woods police department's questions, and those from the bomb squad, and he sighed with resignation when FBI agents Garrison and Pollack arrived.

"Are you ready to go into protective custody now?" Pollack asked, nodding towards the burned-out shell of Bryce's car.

Ciara still hovered by him. Bryce couldn't talk freely while she was around. And since she was a witness, he couldn't dismiss her.

Bryce shook his head. "They missed again."

"Next time they might not," Garrison warned.

Ciara said, "Bryce, maybe you should."

So he'd be a stalking goat staked out for the hunters to pick off at their leisure? Even now, he couldn't say for sure if Steele owned these FBI agents or not. Maybe they'd told him about the rival in order to herd him into protective custody.

He had to stay free and retain enough privacy to play his own double agent game. "I'm on a major case. I can't do my job if I'm in protective custody."

"You can't get Steele off if you're dead," Ciara snapped.

Oh, very good. Bryce wanted to applaud. She'd injected the right amount of outrage in her voice. Of course, if she were working for Steele alone, she'd want him to succeed. *You can't have it both ways, Gannon. She's either for you succeeding, or she wants you dead.* God, he wished he knew which.

"If not protective custody, at least let us assign police protection to you. That might prevent future attempts on your life," Garrison offered.

Bryce looked at his car again. He still ran the risk of any cop being in Steele's employ. Which was better, to worry about an unknown, unseen assassin or to be able to pinpoint someone sent to guard him who might or might not be on Steele's payroll? If the cop was honest, Bryce would still have to keep alert for possible death threats. He was positive Steele could make sure one of his people got the assignment to protect Bryce. But Steele couldn't assure his people's loyalties, not while this power play was happening.

Bryce would go crazy playing these guessing games about the people around him. Better to limit the number.

"I'll think about it," he told the Feds.

Pollack's face flushed with what Bryce thought was anger. Garrison looked like he wanted to argue. Bryce turned and walked back towards the house. The bomb had sapped his meager store of energy. All he wanted was to sit down and breathe, but he had to call for window repairs, a professional cleaning company, his office, his insurance company, and Mrs. McCleary.

Ciara dogged his steps. "Bryce, you're making the wrong choice. You need to listen to the FBI."

He whirled. He needed time to regroup in private where he felt safe. "What I need is for you to interview those witnesses. This trial isn't going to wait while you argue with me."

As he walked away, Bryce could feel Ciara's angry gaze on his back. Tough. But when he reached the kitchen, he began to shake. The last time he'd been caged—during the hazing—Paul, Roger, and Sean had come to his rescue. Paul and Roger were fighting their own cages. Could Sean rescue Bryce by himself? Or was Bryce on his own this time?

· · ·

Ciara watched Bryce walk away, fuming and terrified at the same time—terrified *for him*. What was the matter with him that he wouldn't accept police protection? Whoever wanted him dead meant business.

His face had been a cold, emotionless mask. Did it mean nothing to him that someone was gunning for him? Why did getting Steele acquitted mean more than his life? Was the mobster the key to Bryce getting a judgeship? Surely there were other ways to get elected. And, as she'd told Bryce, he wouldn't be anything if he were dead.

The police gave her permission to drive her dented car away from the scene. She'd have to call her insurance company. But first she needed to make a very important phone call to her boss. A few miles down the road she pulled into a gas station.

Lawrence Baisden was appalled at the news. "It wasn't my intention to send you into the line of fire, Ciara. Come back here until the situation resolves itself. If we need to, we can investigate at a later date."

"You mean abandon Bryce to his fate?" And another thought followed quickly on the heels of the first. "By 'resolves itself' do you mean that if Bryce is killed the point becomes moot?" Was Baisden that cold-blooded?

"That wasn't what I meant. It's too dangerous for you there. I don't want you to become collateral damage."

"I got close to Gannon during his moment of weakness. If I leave now, he won't let me back in. I'm sure of it."

Baisden sighed. "I could order you home."

"You could, but you won't. This is the best chance we have to find out the truth about Gannon's relationship with Steele."

"I know. By the way, I finished the financial check on Gannon. He inherited the house in Grosse Pointe from his parents."

Ciara tried not to name the relief she felt, but something tight in her chest eased. "He said he didn't have any family."

"His parents died in a car crash while he was at the University of Michigan. They were old money, Ciara. So were his grandparents. Gannon was born with a silver spoon in his mouth. He was sent to boarding school when he was twelve. I was surprised he didn't attend Harvard, his father's alma mater.

"He's got family money, so if he's corrupt it's not because someone bought him. His name is good enough to run for judge, but Steele's backing could clinch a seat on the bench."

"So why does a rich boy defend criminals?" Ciara mused.

"That's what I want to know. Keep digging, and watch your back."

"I will."

Ciara hung up feeling a strange sense of jubilation. She'd get to stay and try to figure out the enigma that was Bryce. When had she changed from thinking of him as Gannon to Bryce? And when had his safety become more important to her than her own?

She felt pity for the young boy sent away from his parents. Had he learned to be coldly impassive at boarding school because he was afraid to show he missed his parents? She was losing her impartial perspective.

• • •

"Sean, someone just tried to kill me," Bryce told his friend.

Sean made choking noises into the phone. "What? Are you all right?"

"Bruised and shaken. My car is totaled, though." Bryce sipped hot, sweet tea to settle his nerves and watched the police through the glassless kitchen windows.

"What? Were you driving? What happened?"

Bryce told Sean about the car bomb.

"You need police protection," Sean responded immediately.

"I can't risk it," Bryce admitted. "Adam Steele's reach is everywhere, probably even to the cops."

"You think Steele's trying to kill you? But you're defending him. You're his best chance of acquittal."

"Not Steele. Remember what the Feds said about the power struggle?"

"Then call the Feds."

"Steele probably has contacts there too. There's an FBI office in town. It's probably great to have federal cops on the payroll."

"Talk to those two FBI agents. I don't think they would have told you about Steele's rival if they were on his payroll."

"But how can I be sure?" Bryce told Sean his theory about the Feds.

"Bryce, I thought you got over your trust issues."

Anger sparked inside Bryce, burning away the icy fear. "Don't psychoanalyze me, Sean. You're my friend, not my shrink. Somebody's tried to kill me twice. I think I've got a right to be leery."

There was a pause before Sean spoke again, and then he seemed to choose his words carefully. "Then call another FBI office. Call Washington DC or Quantico. Tell them what you're afraid of."

Would another office pass the buck right back to Detroit? And what if Agents Garrison and Pollack were actually good cops? Then questioning their honesty might ruin them.

When Bryce didn't respond, Sean spoke again. "Bryce, there's another choice."

"What?"

"If you want to hide, I can get you into the sanitarium where I have privileges, anonymously of course. Some famous people have gone there to dry out in the rehab wing."

It was tempting to lose himself among the rich Detroiters whose vices had gotten out of control. But it would be difficult to work there and there'd be no privacy from the other inmates. Still.

"I'll think about it."

"Okay. Do you need anything?"

Bryce needed a friend, someone he could trust implicitly. "Are you doing anything tonight?"

"Um, I have a date."

Disappointment swamped Bryce. "Some other time then."

"No, you want to talk. I want to help. It's just . . . I cancelled on her the first night you were in the hospital."

Oh. Bryce couldn't ask his friend to cancel twice on a woman on his account.

Sean blurted, "I'll reschedule some patients and come over this afternoon. Let me work on it."

"No, your patients need you."

"So do you."

"It's okay, Sean. I'll call Paul or Roger."

Yet when Bryce hung up, he hesitated to call the others. They had problems enough of their own. But they should hear about the bombing from him before they heard it on the news.

His conversations with Paul and Roger, and Christian and Gabrielle too, reassured him. People cared about him and his welfare. Gabrielle offered to come touch the remains of his car to see if she could psychically identify the bomber.

That hadn't occurred to him. He knew what she could do but he'd been an evidence man so long he didn't consider other avenues.

Unfortunately, his car had been removed to the CSI crime lab and was off-limits to Gabrielle. Bryce didn't know what he'd do if she got a description anyway, unless the major crimes unit could identify the person that way. And then what? Without evidence, they couldn't convict. He knew all about getting the bad guys off on lack of evidence.

Crap. He never thought he'd be on this side of the fence wanting to convict on circumstantial evidence. Guilt ate at him like acid in his gut. How helpless those victims must have felt when big bad Bryce Gannon used the law against them. Hell, he'd loved the law until now, loved its logic, its purity, its structure. Now he saw how it was used to perpetrate injustice. He'd become the bad guy. He felt sick. It hadn't been his intention to harm innocent people.

They said payback was hell.

CHAPTER 7

Bryce found security in the familiar. He'd never stopped to consider it before, but ensconced in his office for the first time in more than a week, he felt safe. Even though the ricin attack had occurred here, this was where his armor was strongest. His employees knew only the persistent winner without weakness or vulnerability. He'd built a firm foundation here, and thick walls. His staff had welcomed him back with inquiries after his health and he'd assured them of his recovery without inviting further personal conversation.

His home was nearly back to normal and Mrs. McCleary was overseeing the work's completion. He was amazed once more how fast money got work done. He'd spent the evening with Paul and Roger, so he was feeling his usual self once more.

Bryce suffered his first moment of disorientation that everything in his office was out of place, but he firmed his will and got to work.

The second moment came when Ciara entered his office. She didn't belong here in her red blouse and red and black flame-patterned skirt. He'd worked with her in the hospital and in his home office, both informal situations where he'd allowed her liberties he wouldn't dream of granting his employees. Now that he was operating from his usual position of strength and power, he needed to have the same detached relationship with her that he had with everyone else in his office.

She scrutinized him without trying to appear to do so. "How did you get here today?"

"The same way you did."

"I doubt that." Her dark brows pinched. "Why won't you tell me?"

"Because this is my office. I don't engage in idle chatter with my employees."

Ciara smiled. "Ah. You're the king and this is your kingdom."

Bryce fought an answering smile but one corner of his mouth quirked up a little. "Something like that. I take it you have the interviews from yesterday?"

She handed him her typed notes. "The second one, Harold Andryzak, recently underwent quadruple bypass. I had to track him down in the hospital."

"Is he able to testify?"

"He says he will be."

"Trial starts Monday. If he doesn't appear in court—"

"Mr. Andryzak knows that and he plans to appear."

"He might have complications or a relapse."

Ciara glared at him. "He has just as much to prove by coming to court from his sickbed as you do."

"I didn't come from my sickbed."

"No? Two days out of the hospital is hardly enough time to recover your strength."

"I'm not going to argue about this with you. This is my firm. If you want to continue to work here . . . "

Ciara drew herself erect, lifting her chin. "I'll get to the rest of the files." Then she walked out, her stride as regal as a queen.

Bryce's office was emptier without her in it. She stimulated his brain when they were together—and other parts more southerly. Recovering, ha.

He settled back in his chair to read through dozens of depositions. A few hours later he heard raised voices. Since that rarely happened in his firm, he left his office to investigate.

"The police should be vetting packages before they come here," Ciara told someone with some heat. Bryce should have known she'd be involved.

"It's not addressed to the company. It's personal. Besides, I've seen this company's name before." Sharron, his office manager, explained, gripping a box to her mid-section. She was a short, stout, meticulously groomed brunette in her mid-forties. "Mr. Gannon orders his shoes from there."

Shoes. His new hand-stitched leather shoes had arrived in record time. Money did get things done faster.

"I think we should call the bomb squad," Ciara insisted.

Like hell he was going to lose another pair of shoes. Bryce stormed down the hall to where the two women stood facing off in front of the reception desk. He grabbed the box from Sharron. Yes, the company was where he'd ordered the shoes only a few days ago.

"Mr. Gannon," the receptionist cried, startled.

"Bryce, don't take any chances," Ciara warned.

"Thanks, Sharron." Bryce nodded to his office manager. He spun on his heel, happy to have saved the shoes from a dunking or worse.

"Bryce, you don't know what's in there," Ciara protested, following him.

"Shoes. I ordered them." He couldn't wait to put them on. The old pair he wore now was uncomfortable.

Snatching his letter opener from his desk drawer, Bryce pried open the box and lifted the lid.

"Bryce, at least—"

The muffled boom shot white powder into Bryce's face, into his nose and open mouth, and rocked him back on his feet gasping and scrubbing desperately at his face, trying to clear his eyes. God, not more ricin! His heart pounded in his ears. The powder tasted like paste. He needed to spit. He tried not to inhale.

"Bryce!" Ciara screamed. She was covered in a fine mist of white powder.

Bryce gasped for air and his lungs constricted with the powder. He began coughing and couldn't stop.

He couldn't catch his breath or draw in enough air. Fear and panic danced a dizzying whirl in his mind. He remembered how much it hurt last time, and that wasn't a direct hit. This time he'd gotten the full dose. His breath whistled as he drew it in. His lungs burned with the lack of air. Slowly he sank to the thick carpet, clutching the desk to keep upright.

God, it was just like last time. Only this time he was going to die for sure.

"Call nine-one-one!" Ciara screamed. "Bryce, where's your oxygen?"

Bryce couldn't speak. Why did Ciara think oxygen would help, anyway? Through the white cloud that slowly drifted to the carpet he noted his staff filling the doorway of his office. Were they as terrified as he was? He hadn't even gotten to use the second chance he'd been given. And he really wanted to.

It seemed the familiar wasn't so safe after all.

• • •

Ciara watched Bryce gasp for breath and felt helpless. Her mind and heart were racing. "Oxygen. He needs oxygen," she snapped at the paralyzed staff. "Look for an oxygen tank."

One young blonde woman broke free to search the room on the outskirts of the white cloud.

How long would it be before Ciara was gasping like Bryce? She'd coughed a couple of times when the powder first hit her, but nothing more. Had she been far enough away to avoid a fatal dose? Or was she going to die more slowly? She didn't want to die.

"There's no oxygen tank," the blonde reported, wringing her hands. She sounded near hysteria.

Hadn't Bryce brought it to work? Damn his pride. "Try to find some in this building."

"Nine-one-one's coming," Sharron reported in a breathless voice. "Oh, God, it *was* a bomb." She moaned like a dying thing.

How long did a fatal dose of ricin take to kill someone? Would Bryce die right here as they watched? His blue eyes were wild as he struggled to breathe.

"Bryce, help is coming."

What more could she say? Ciara covered his hand with hers where he gripped the desk edge. He turned his hand under hers and squeezed in a death grip.

She winced at that description.

Oh, where was help? If they could only make it in time. She knelt beside him on the plush carpet and he gave her a grateful look.

The minutes stretched out into eons, punctuated by the tortured shriek of air whistling in and out of Bryce's lungs. His hand grew clammy. Sweat broke out on his upper lip, beading the white powder to paste. His lips had a blue cast to them, like she'd seen in the ICU. He sank to the carpet as his strength faded.

Shouts came from the hallway, excited babble, and then the EMTs surged through the doorway. Ciara had never been so happy to see anyone in her life. A little of the tension eased out of her muscles.

"Letter bomb," Sharron informed them.

"It might be ricin poison," Ciara added as she stood and moved out of the way.

The EMTs surrounded Bryce, laying him flat, getting an oxygen mask on him. They donned masks over their mouths and noses.

"He just got out of the hospital last week from a ricin letter bomb," Ciara added.

"God, this is the guy?" one EMT asked.

She nodded.

"You were in the bomb's path too?" the EMT asked, looking her over.

"Yes, but I don't feel any symptoms."

"Maybe you'd better sit down, to be safe. We'll get to you in a minute."

The EMTs worked vigorously over Bryce. They opened his shirt and attached monitor leads. Ciara could almost count the half minutes by the calming of Bryce's breathing. When the horrible wheezing stopped, her heart hitched, but Bryce's eyes were open and following the activity around him.

She remembered he'd said the last time he'd been unconscious when he reached the hospital. Would that be soon?

Police officers entered the room and shooed the frightened employees outside. Ciara heard Sharron taking charge. One policeman knelt next to her.

"Were you contaminated, miss?"

"Yes, but I feel all right. I was trying to stop Bryce from opening the box. I wanted him to call the bomb squad."

Why hadn't she insisted more firmly? Why hadn't she grabbed his arm? She was a strong woman. She could have stopped him. She didn't want him hurt or killed.

The thought startled her. A week ago she wouldn't have cared less.

Bryce stared at her until an EMT moved to block her view.

"Can you walk me through what happened?" the officer coaxed.

The EMTs gently loaded Bryce onto a gurney.

"Can it wait? We need to get to the hospital. The box is on his desk." She waved in that direction.

The EMTs paused by her. "You'd better come with us."

"I'll follow you to the hospital," the cop said.

It was a worrisome ride in the ambulance with the siren screaming. Ciara wanted to scream too. She wanted to shake off the tension that tightened her muscles and the fear that made her nearly nauseous. Thank God it was a short trip. Bryce was wheeled right into an exam room.

"Bryce Gannon, aged thirty-nine, possible ricin poisoning. Letter bomb," the EMT explained. "My station brought him in last week for the same thing."

Medical staff converged on Bryce and a woman in blue scrubs ran from the room, probably to get Bryce's records.

"You'll have to wait outside, miss," a nurse told her.

"She was exposed too," the EMT said.

"I feel all right," Ciara objected. "Help Bryce."

"Ricin is toxic. I was here the last time this man was brought in, so I know. We need to check you over," the nurse insisted.

"I read about ricin when I went to work for Mr. Gannon. If the symptoms haven't already set in, I have hours until it's critical. I can wait."

"All right. But stay here. We don't want you out in the waiting room."

Ciara watched them cut Bryce's clothes off, and winced. Bryce wasn't going to like that.

How strange that she thought he'd survive this attack too. Maybe because he was still conscious. Odd, he'd gotten only a partial exposure last time. This time he'd gotten the powder right in his face. Had it been a more concentrated poison last time?

A tech ran out with a sample. Ciara prayed that it was less powerful ricin. If, no, when, Bryce recuperated this time, she'd insist that he have police protection.

Since when did she have any power over him? She decided she'd call Lawrence Baisden and have him wield the power of the Attorney General's office.

In a few minutes the tech slammed back through the swinging doors. "It's not ricin."

"What? Well then what is it?" the E.R. doctor snapped.

"Flour mostly. Somebody's playing a sick joke on this guy."

"But he couldn't breathe," Ciara protested while her mind whirled. A joke? This wasn't funny.

The woman in blue scrubs followed the tech in with a medical chart. "Mr. Gannon has reduced lung capacity, like COPD. He's on bronchodilators. Any extreme level of stress would bring on an asthma-like attack."

She leaned over Bryce. "Mr. Gannon, why didn't you use your inhaler when you couldn't breathe?"

Ciara moved closer to hear Bryce's answer.

"Thought—it—was—ricin." His voice rasped and rattled like stones in a metal can.

"Dr. Khalil is his pulmonologist," the woman continued.

"Page him," the doctor ordered. "Get him here so we can find out if his patient's had a relapse."

Ciara sagged against the wall, letting out her breath. Bryce would live. But that sick bastard who'd sent the bomb would see the inside of a jail cell if she had anything to say about it.

When the staff was done poking and prodding Bryce and word came that Dr. Khalil was on his way, Ciara found herself alone with Bryce. She moved to his side. Hesitantly, she took his hand. It was cool to the touch. He squeezed in return.

"How do you feel?" she asked.

"Lousy." The word was muffled through the oxygen mask.

"You're alive."

"Yeah."

His stare was intense. He signaled her lower. When she leaned over him, he moved his mask and kissed her. He tasted of flour and antiseptic and man. Ciara felt a thrill run through her that traveled to her toes and curled them. Her pulse went haywire.

When the kiss ended, Ciara pulled back gently so Bryce could replace the oxygen mask. "What was that for?"

"For holding my hand."

She frowned. That made no sense.

"For wanting me alive," he croaked.

Why would he think she wanted him dead?

"Excuse me, the doctor said it was okay to come in," FBI agent Garrison said from the doorway. He wore a navy suit. Agent Pollack, also wearing a dark suit, followed him in.

"Miss Alafita," Garrison's dark eyes were full of keen interest and intelligent speculation.

She moved away from Bryce giving the agents better access to the gurney.

"The doctor said it might be difficult for you to talk, so I'll try to limit the questions to yes or no answers," Garrison said to Bryce.

"We've been to the crime scene," Agent Pollack explained. "The doctor said it's not ricin, which explains the note that came with the package." He held it up in its clear evidence bag where Bryce could see it.

Bryce frowned.

The agent showed it to Ciara.

Walk away now or you're dead.

CHAPTER 8

"'Walk away now or you're dead' is pretty clear," Agent Garrison said.

So the letter bomb had only been a warning? That made no sense. Bryce voiced his doubts. "Two real bombs and then a fake? Hoax?"

"Rather an elaborate hoax," Agent Pollack said. "The box you received had a typed FedEx airbill on it. An overseas airbill. Someplace in Italy."

Bryce's shoes came from Italy. "Shoes? In the box?"

Pollack glanced at his partner before answering. "No. Why did you think there were?"

Bryce slid the oxygen mask aside. "Ordered them. Three days ago."

"How?" Pollack demanded.

"Internet."

Pollack nodded. "They're tracking your computer movements trying to get to you."

"Who?" Ciara asked.

Bryce couldn't shake his head in time to prevent Pollack from answering. "Adam Steele's rival."

"Rival?" she choked. "You think this is over the Steele case?"

"It's the likeliest possibility," Garrison said.

"That's crazy. Attacking the defense attorney doesn't assure Steele goes to jail. He'll just get another lawyer. Why not just kill Steele?"

"He's probably as well guarded as the president of the United States," Garrison told her. "The chances of getting to him—and getting away alive—are slim. Killing Mr. Gannon, or any other defense attorney, has a better chance of succeeding."

His partner continued, "Now they're trying to scare you off the case."

"Mind games." Ciara shuddered.

"Russian roulette," Garrison agreed. "Will the next time be an empty threat—?"

"Or a bullet," Bryce rasped.

Ciara gasped. "Bryce needs protection before it comes to that."

"Mr. Gannon," Agent Pollack began, "You've refused protection each time it's been offered. We're offering again."

"Take it, Bryce," Ciara begged.

Bryce sighed and nodded. "No safe house."

"You'd be safest there," Garrison argued.

"Can't work there."

"Miss Alafita can bring you anything you need from your office," Garrison said.

Bryce looked at Ciara. What she knew, Steele's organization knew. He couldn't caution her not to tell anyone but Steele without her knowing that he knew her secret.

Although now Ciara knew about Steele's rival. It wouldn't take long for Steele to shake out the traitor and it would either be bloody or the person would disappear like Jimmy Hoffa had. Bryce wondered if the Feds knew the person's name, but he wouldn't seal the man or woman's death warrant by handing the name to Ciara.

"They'd follow her," he responded to Garrison's offer. "No safe house." His voice had grown progressively hoarser as he talked. Now a coughing spasm gripped him. Afterwards he felt spent . . . and angry. Rage was the only warmth he felt in this cold, sterile room. Damn Steele's whole organization.

"You'll accept protection though?" Pollack insisted.

Bryce nodded. "Federal." The word was nearly soundless.

Pollack and Garrison exchanged a look. Then Pollack glanced at Ciara. "Would you excuse us for a few minutes, please?"

She looked ready to protest, glancing at the three of them. But then she turned and left the room.

"You don't trust the local cops?" Garrison asked, his voice low, his gaze sharply incisive.

"No."

"You have proof? Names?" Pollack demanded, pen poised over his notepad.

Bryce shook his head.

"Yet you can still defend Steele," Garrison said, "Knowing what you do."

"Or suspecting it," his partner added.

Bryce kept silent. He'd only said what he had to in order to stay alive.

Frustrated anger fired Garrison's brown eyes. "We've got work to do to set up your protection. For now we'll leave you with the cop who followed you from your office. I don't think he wants you dead, if he's corrupt."

Cops had swarmed in and out of Bryce's life since the ricin bomb, each one unknown. What was one more? But he debated saying aloud the rest of his doubts. The FBI agents were nearly at the door when he spoke.

"Feds can be bought too."

Garrison drilled him with a look. A muscle bunched in his jaw. Clearly he wanted to ask for names but knew he'd get none.

Pollack didn't suffer from a lack of words. "You're sending us back to our office wondering if any of the people we work with are dirty. That's low even for a lawyer who defends scum."

Garrison tried again. "You could turn States' evidence. Tell what you know. You'd go into Witness Protection."

Bryce heard the click of heels outside his door. He couldn't let Ciara report this conversation to Steele. "Can't help you."

Garrison's eyes snapped with anger and Pollack's narrowed with disgust when they left. They passed Ciara on their way out. She watched them go, frowning a little.

"They don't look happy."

Bryce settled his head back against the gurney and held the oxygen mask over his mouth, inhaling as deeply as he could. She was so easy on the eyes. Too bad she was a spy.

"Don't like my choice of client."

She moved closer to him. "It's a popular opinion."

Bryce shrugged. The tightness in his chest eased a little. He moved the mask aside. "Take the day off. I'm not going back to the office." He took a drag of oxygen. "I'll go home when I'm released."

"I can drive you home."

"Not necessary. Go home. Tomorrow's July Fourth. See your family. I'll be in the office on Thursday."

"Okay." But she frowned at him, looking him over. "Are you sure you'll be all right here by yourself?"

"A cop is outside."

"That's not what I meant."

"My friend Sean is coming."

"Oh. Okay." She looked slightly relieved. "I'll see you the day after tomorrow."

He nodded. Still she hesitated. Thoughts flitted through her expressive dark eyes, and then her chin jerked up. "See you." And she left.

They were barely even friends, so why did he wish she'd kissed him good-bye?

• • •

Ciara called Baisden as soon as she left the hospital, relaying everything she knew. He insisted she stick to Bryce like glue from now on.

"Gannon knows about police corruption. This is what I'd hoped to uncover." Excitement laced his voice. "Keep your eyes and ears open around him and Steele. Learn everything you can.

"If Steele owns the cops, Gannon should have accepted protection immediately," Baisden mused. "That's an anomaly."

"But if someone is making a move in Steele's organization, Bryce wouldn't know if a person was working for Steele or his rival." No wonder he hadn't wanted police protection.

"True." Ciara could almost hear Baisden thinking. "Gannon should be off balance. Maybe we can push him over to our side. Is he?"

"It's hard to read Bryce. He keeps his emotions firmly under control."

"Has he warned Steele that you know of?"

"Not in my presence. In fact, he's never spoken to Steele when I've been around. That's strange."

"Maybe he doesn't trust you yet. He's keeping his dealings with Steele private."

"But it's public knowledge he's defending the man."

"But anything else between them is secret. I need you to win the man's trust enough to find out what he's hiding."

"That won't be easy. Bryce keeps his own counsel."

"There'll never be a better time. Three attempts on his life in two weeks have got to have him thinking about his mortality. He won't want some of his secrets to die with him if the next attempt succeeds."

"Offer myself as a confessional?"

"Whatever it takes. Get that information, Ciara."

"Yes, sir."

Ciara hung up, slipped the phone into her purse and stared at the emergency entrance. Her hand rose to touch two fingers to her lips as she remembered Bryce's kiss. Her heart danced with excitement. It had been unexpected, and had thrilled her. But why he should feel the need to thank her for the simple act of holding his hand made what Baisden asked seem like treachery.

She knew how important it was to unmask corrupt law officers. But did Bryce have to get ground up to obtain that information?

Ciara hesitated before calling a cab. She didn't like leaving Bryce alone. After the letter bomb exploded, none of his employees had dared come near him. She'd been the first to reach out to him, and not because she'd already been exposed to whatever had been in the bomb. She couldn't stand to see him suffer.

• • •

Sean arrived at the same time as Dr. Khalil. Sean's brown hair stood up in tufts like he'd pulled on it on his way here. "My God, what happened?"

"It wasn't ricin," Bryce forestalled Sean's incipient heart failure. His remaining hoarseness probably didn't help Sean's state, although his friend let out a loud sigh of relief.

But it made Dr. Khalil frown. "But you inhaled something."

"Yeah." Bryce told them in brief, terse words. In retrospect his reaction sounded ridiculous. He ended with, "There's nothing wrong that rest won't cure."

"I'd like to run tests to be sure," Dr. Khalil said.

God, not more torture. "I feel fine." Well, that was an exaggeration, but compared to the ricin attack Bryce felt like a million bucks. He looked to Sean for his friend's support.

But Sean frowned. "Bryce, Dr. Khalil is right. I know I'd feel better if the hospital checked you out."

"It wasn't ricin. I'm all right."

"The tests won't take too long, Bryce," Dr. Khalil argued. "I can't in good conscience release you without them."

With bad grace Bryce conceded defeat. But the tests took hours, mostly spent waiting, and then more time waiting for Dr. Khalil to return to examine the results. Which showed exactly what Bryce had said. His lungs were irritated. They needed to rest. *He* needed to rest.

Sean argued for Bryce to stay overnight, but Bryce had had enough. First the bomber had derailed his planned day, and then Sean and Dr. Khalil had hijacked the rest of his day. Bryce was going home to his own damn bed.

As he exited the room, the FBI agent on duty detached himself from the wall and attached himself to Bryce.

Damn. His life was no longer his own.

CHAPTER 9

Ciara had washed her clothes, stocked the kitchen of her extended-stay hotel and was just deciding what to do for dinner when her cell phone rang. When she saw her mother's number on the caller ID, Ciara sighed and braced herself.

"Hello, Mama."

"*M'hija*, tomorrow Carmen is having a holiday cookout. Your brothers and their wives and children will be there. You hardly get to see your nieces and nephews. I thought now that you are so close you could come even though it is mid-week."

Ah, the mother guilt trip. It was easier to ignore when Ciara lived an hour-and-a-half away. "I don't know if I'll be free or not."

"What are you going to do? Work?" That last word dripped with derision. "It is bad enough you do not have children of your own, but to ignore your nieces and nephews? Ignore your brothers and sister and their wives and husband? All because you are angry at me?"

Ciara sighed again. "I'm not angry at you, Mama."

"I did not raise you to lie, Ciara. And shame on you for staying away. You have been in town for days."

And working. But her mother didn't want to hear that. "All right, I'll be there. What time?"

"Noon. I know you do not cook—"

"I'll stop at the store and pick something up."

"Oh, Ciara." Two words sure could carry a load of mother guilt and quiet despair.

"I'll bring ice cream for the children. Everyone likes ice cream."

"Very well. I will see you tomorrow."

Ciara hoped there wouldn't be any matchmaking. She didn't know which was worse—inviting any single men to the family gatherings or listening to her mother castigate her life choices and lack of husband and children.

But the next morning as Ciara stood on Bryce's doorstep, she had second thoughts about the crazy plan she'd hatched in the desperate aftermath of last night's phone call. She had no idea what she was doing inviting Bryce to a family picnic. She took a deep breath and rang his doorbell anyway.

A blonde woman opened the door. Ciara gaped. Had Bryce finally found a girlfriend to replace Monique? Or was this the possible affair that had caused Monique to dump Bryce? Disappointment and anger stabbed at Ciara. The beautiful day dimmed.

"Can I help you?" The woman's voice was businesslike. In fact, her suit was businesslike too, in a severe way.

"I'm here to see Bryce."

"Who are you?"

"Ciara Alafita."

"Just a minute." And the blonde woman shut the door in Ciara's face with a click.

Ciara stared at the door, perplexed. It couldn't be a girlfriend. Bryce liked his blondes gorgeous. That woman had seemed like a butler, protecting the house from riffraff.

Protecting the house.

Ciara could have kicked herself for her stupidity. Relief almost made her sag. The woman was a federal agent.

Finally the door opened again and the blonde stepped back to let Ciara in. "Mr. Gannon's in his office. I understand you know the way."

"Yes, I do." Ciara should have known he'd be working. She proceeded to Bryce's office.

Whatever she'd been going to say flew out of her mind as she rounded the doorway and saw him sitting behind his desk. He wore a red polo shirt that fit snug to his wide shoulders and firm chest. Her mouth dried. Her body felt achy. His suits disguised his body's athletic power. She'd seen his bare chest yesterday, but there was something mouthwatering about a man in a tight shirt.

Bryce looked up from his legal tablet and caught her gawking at him like a teenage girl gushing over a pop star. "I gave you the day off." Yesterday's hoarseness was gone.

"I know." She stepped fully into the room.

Bryce's gaze swept over her red knit sundress and sandals. His once-over lingered and warmed her. His gaze rose to meet hers once more. There was a hint of a smile on his chiseled lips.

"That's a different look for you."

"And you as well." She smiled at him in invitation. "I'm wearing this for my mother."

"I won't keep you from your family get-together. Did you need something?"

"I'd like you to come with me."

Bryce didn't catch his momentary shock fast enough and Ciara savored the ability to prick his perfect composure.

"Go with you?"

"Sure. You need to escape this house and the case for a few hours."

Bryce laid his pen down and leaned back in his chair. "It's nice of you to offer, but I don't intrude on employees' family time."

"You won't be intruding. In fact, with you there my mother will be on her very best behavior and I won't have to take any heat."

"I see. An ulterior motive."

"Bryce, I really want you to come. It will do you good to relax for a few hours. And my mother is a great cook. Although our holiday food is a little non-traditional. You may have noticed I'm Hispanic."

"I've noticed. So the food has a Latin influence?"

"Definitely. You'll come?"

His gaze drifted behind her. "I'm not sure I want to put your family in danger."

"Nobody would expect you there, so it's perfect. Like hiding in plain sight."

"Let me see what Agent Andrews thinks." Bryce rose. He wore long khaki shorts that made his lean legs look longer.

Ciara practically gaped at his brown leather sandals, but she refrained from commenting. Of course he relaxed at home. When she wasn't there.

She followed him to the kitchen where they found the agent drinking a Diet Coke.

"Miss Alafita would like me to go to her family's house for the Fourth," Bryce said. "Do you have any security objections?"

"Is it inside or out?" Andrews asked.

"Out," Ciara answered.

"Family only or will there be strangers?"

"I hope it's only family."

"What do you mean?" Andrews asked sharply.

Ciara saw that Bryce was just as focused on her. She felt her cheeks warm. "My mother likes to matchmake."

She felt Bryce's attention intensify.

But Andrews relaxed. "How many people will be there?"

"My mother. My sister, her husband, and their three children. My two brothers, their wives, and their six children."

"Nine children." Bryce looked thoughtful.

"That won't be a problem, will it?" Ciara asked.

Bryce drew himself up to tower over her. "No."

"Good. Agent Andrews?"

"I see no problem. Children like me."

"What?" Ciara blurted.

Andrews's eyes chilled. "Protective custody isn't like day care where you can choose whether to drop your child off or not. I take my job—and this threat—very seriously. I go wherever Mr. Gannon goes."

Ciara looked between Andrews and Bryce. She'd thought only to ease the strain on Bryce. She fought a totally inappropriate feeling of disappointment.

"How stupid of me. I'm sorry. I didn't think."

Andrews's stiff posture eased and her eyes thawed. "It's not a problem. I can sit in the car outside the house."

"Nonsense. It's the Fourth of July. You'll join the celebration. Um, do you have anything casual to wear?"

"I'm on duty," Andrews reminded her.

"I'd really like not to have to explain protective custody to my family."

On the drive to her sister's house in Royal Oak, Ciara debated calling ahead to warn her family that she was bringing guests, but she decided she'd rather surprise them.

Ciara glanced at Bryce in the passenger's seat. He looked at ease, as though she hadn't seen how much he enjoyed being the one in control behind the wheel mere days ago. Maybe it was his casual attire that made him seem more . . . approachable, less tightly in control. The warm red color made him seem less cold. She wrenched her gaze from him.

She thought a brief overview might be in order before they arrived. "We're going to my sister Carmen's house. She and her husband Esteban live there with their three children and my mother. My mother is separated from my father, so try not to mention him."

Bryce gave her a sharp, inquisitive look.

"Any other mine fields to avoid?" Andrews asked.

Other than that she was Carmen's older, unmarried sister? "None that I can think of." Or wanted to admit to. Oh, God, what was she getting herself into?

...

Ciara pulled her red Toyota Camry into the driveway of an older white two-story house. The flowerbeds were a riot of blooming colors. A child's purple bike lay discarded on the front walk. The driveway already contained two minivans.

Bryce watched her draw in a long breath and lift her chin before she exited the car.

Agent Andrews put a hand on his arm. "Let me check it out first."

She climbed out of the car. She'd let down her wheat blonde hair and changed into a white tank top and navy shorts from the gym bag she carried in her car. Her gun was tucked into the sweater she had tied around her waist.

Bryce breathed out and forced himself to relax. He'd asked for the protection. Now he had to accept it. But he wished he could have come here alone with Ciara. He thought she might relax and slip up around her family. He might even learn her true relationship with Steele.

Agent Andrews opened his door. "All clear."

Bryce stepped out to meet Ciara's dark gaze. He couldn't read her expression.

As they'd agreed beforehand, Bryce took Agent Andrews' arm. Ciara led them on the concrete sidewalk between the house and garage, her plastic grocery bags swinging from both hands.

"Aunt Ciara," a trio of dark-haired girls trilled. They grabbed her hands and dragged her towards the back yard.

A mob of dark-eyed, dark-haired people met them. Slowly everyone turned to stare.

A thickened woman in her early fifties set a dish on a table and wiped her hands on her green apron as she hurried towards them.

"Ciara, you brought guests." Was that gentle censure in the woman's voice?

"Mama, I've brought my boss—"

Her mother gasped. "Your boss?"

"Mama, this is Bryce Gannon and his girlfriend Sonya Andrews. Bryce, Sonya, my mother Ascension Salazar Alafita."

Ciara's mother seemed speechless so Bryce took her hand. "Thank you for opening your home to us, Mrs. Alafita. Sonya and I hadn't made any plans, so when your daughter graciously asked us to join your festivities we accepted."

Mrs. Alafita smiled and Bryce saw where Ciara got her beauty. "I have never met Ciara's boss before. But she has lived far away for so long."

"You must be very happy to have her home again," Bryce said.

"We still see so little of her."

"I'm settling in and looking for a place to live," Ciara explained.

Interesting. So Ciara's excuse for moving home wasn't the whole truth.

"It is time you were settling down," her mother said.

Well, Ciara had told them the truth about that, at least.

"Let me introduce you to the rest of my family." Ciara led them to the large group.

Bryce met the hostess and her husband, Carmen and Esteban Hernandez. Bryce was startled to find Carmen nearly a decade younger than Ciara. He knew Ciara was thirty-two, but this young woman couldn't be more than mid-twenties. Ciara had nearly a head of height on Carmen and was more beautiful. Strange, then, that her much younger sister had married first.

"You're the one injured by the letter bomb!" Carmen exclaimed.

He forced himself to relax. He'd known the story would haunt him for months, maybe years. "Yes." Thank God yesterday's attack had been suppressed. He wondered about that for a moment.

Carmen shook her head and pursed her lips. "It just goes to show you can't believe what you read in the papers. They said you'd nearly been killed. But you look fine."

Bryce wasn't about to divulge his injury to strangers, or that he'd spent most of yesterday in the hospital.

"I'm fine."

Carmen shooed children out of the way so the other adults could meet Bryce. Ciara's brothers were closer to her age but older than her. Carlos Junior looked a lot like Ciara and shared her height. His wife Eloisa was a round dumpling of a woman who looked like she wore a perpetual smile.

Ciara's other brother Francisco studied Bryce as they shook hands. "I never thought Ciara would give up the Attorney General's office, and especially not to practice defense law. When I heard, I thought . . . " He looked from Bryce to Agent Andrews to Ciara. "Well, I don't know what I thought."

Bryce became more convinced that Steele had ordered Ciara to Bryce's side. What hold did the racketeer have over her? Was it her family? Ciara didn't behave like a woman acting under threat. Bryce couldn't see a long-distance love affair between Steele and Ciara. What would make a woman sell her soul to the devil?

The Hernandez's yard contained a swing set, a vegetable garden, and a profusion of blooming flowers surrounding a statue of the Virgin Mary. Bryce, Agent Andrews, and Ciara settled at a wooden picnic table with plates loaded with tamales, black beans and rice, and the best enchiladas Bryce had ever tasted.

"These are wonderful," he exclaimed.

Ciara's mother beamed. "A family recipe passed down through five generations of Salazar women. I have taught Carmen and my daughters-in-law to make it." She gave Ciara a telling look.

Francisco's wife Nina piped up. "Ciara is a working woman, Mama. She doesn't have time to cook."

"Even working women have to eat," Mrs. Alafita said. "Look at how thin Ciara is. I do not believe she makes time to eat." She tsked. "Too much time working."

Bryce thought Ciara exactly the right shape. She had curves in all the right places and what she did to his libido . . . well, he couldn't think about that in this company.

"*Abuela*, someone's here," one of the children cried.

Agent Andrews reached towards her weapon. Bryce stiffened as everyone at the table spun to look toward the yard's entrance. A Latino in his late thirties glanced over the assemblage.

The man spotted Ciara and strode toward her.

"Mama, you didn't," Ciara whispered.

Ah, enlightenment dawned and Bryce relaxed.

Mrs. Alafita rose, beaming. "I am so glad you could come. Ciara, this is Juan Mendoza. His mama and I go to church together."

Ciara rose and Bryce could see the reluctance in the stiff line of her back. "It's nice to meet you, Mr. Mendoza—"

"Miss Alafita." The man practically fawned over Ciara. "Please call me Juan."

"Juan. Would you like to have a seat?"

Mrs. Alafita made a production of making room next to Ciara. Up close Juan's soft, sallow skin suggested a sedentary life indoors.

"What do you do for a living, Juan?" Bryce asked.

Juan blinked away from Ciara and smiled. "I run an Internet company, Cesar.com. We're in our fifth year and growing exponentially."

"What do you sell?" Ciara inquired with polite interest.

"Oh, I don't sell things. I'm a connector, a liaison. I bring people together."

"Like a matchmaker?" Carmen asked.

"No, no." Juan made negating motions with his hands. "People who need things. Like yesterday a man in Chile needed to place his cousin with an Ohio grower. I made it happen."

"Oh, job placement."

"It's much more than that. I help people find products, places to live, places to vacation, animals, lost relatives."

Carmen frowned. "Is there much of a market for that?"

"We made fifty thousand dollars last year."

Mrs. Alafita beamed from Juan to Ciara.

"Where is your office located?" Ciara asked.

Juan looked sheepish. "We're still small yet. It's in my mother's basement. She's my business partner, you see. Silent partner."

Bryce nearly choked. Ciara looked like she was having a similar problem.

"Juan is a good son," Mrs. Alafita said, her enthusiasm growing as she spoke. "He provides for his widowed mother and keeps her company while making her feel useful in taking care of him."

"My mother would love to cook for a family," Juan said. "She would welcome my wife and children into her house with open arms."

Ciara sputtered, coughing into her napkin. "What a convenient arrangement."

Juan's smile broadened. "Isn't it?"

• • •

Ciara was forced to listen to Juan's detailed stories while her family conversed with Bryce and Agent Andrews. Ciara couldn't help comparing the two men—Bryce so independent and self-contained to Juan tied to his mother's apron strings. Bryce hadn't lived with his mother since he was twelve. Bryce functioned well in society while Juan wouldn't leave his basement and deal directly with people. She'd found out the two men were nearly the same age, but they couldn't be more different inside than they were on the outside. She found Bryce compelling, but Juan made her want to run away.

Was it that Juan reminded her of her family and their Latino problems? She couldn't be sure.

Agent Andrews moved her hand on Bryce's arm, attracting Ciara's attention. She hated the way Sonya's little touches conveyed her part as being with Bryce, leaving Ciara to Juan's advances. Ciara had asked Bryce to this picnic. He was supposed to be with her. She wanted to claw Sonya's eyes out.

She shook herself. Bryce wasn't her anything, except her temporary boss. She had no right to be jealous of Sonya's playacting.

"Papa, he's a bad man." Carmen's youngest son, Federico, pointed at Bryce, his high-pitched voice slicing through the conversation. Silence followed in its wake.

Esteban scrambled to his feet and gathered his little son in his arms. "What nonsense is this? Mr. Gannon is our guest. Apologize to him."

"But, Papa, he has the smokes in his pocket. You said they were bad. He's a bad man."

Esteban turned to Bryce, his face flushing. "I'm sorry. We're teaching our children not to smoke. It's okay if you do."

Bryce frowned. "I don't smoke."

Federico pointed. "In his pocket."

Like a blind man, Bryce slid his hand up his chest until he encountered the bulge in his pocket. His inhaler. Only because she was watching him closely did Ciara see the look of almost despair that flitted through Bryce's eyes. Her heart ached for him. He pulled out the round object.

"I don't smoke," he explained to the child. "This is to help me breathe. It's an inhaler filled with medicine."

"Why do you have trouble breathing?" Federico asked in his piping voice.

Esteban looked horrified. "Hush, Fico." He turned to Bryce. "I'm so sorry. I didn't know you'd been injured that badly. And you were trying to downplay it."

"It's all right. He's just a child trying to do what his parents taught him was right." Bryce turned to the boy. "Someone poisoned me. It got into my lungs. I was very sick for a while, but I'm getting better. If my lungs bother me, I use this." He tapped the inhaler.

"And the medicine makes you all better?" Federico asked.

"When I use it, yes." Bryce slid the inhaler back into his pocket.

Ciara wondered if she was the only one who'd caught Bryce's evasion.

There was a stilted silence until a group of children came running up to their table yelling, "We want ice cream!"

Ciara retrieved the ice cream novelties from the freezer and handed them out. Agent Andrews had her hand on Bryce's forearm again. Ciara longed to be the one to comfort him. She shook her head to dispel that thought. He didn't need comfort. He wasn't diminished by his condition.

• • •

Bryce seethed inside until they could leave. He didn't want anyone's pity and he didn't like that the only thing people remembered about him was that he'd been poisoned. He was so much more than a victim. He didn't like appearing weak or vulnerable in front of people especially with his own personal protection on his arm. In his job, that was fatal to his cases.

He'd been feeling normal again, just a guy and his girlfriend at a picnic. In a split second that had been ruined. Ciara's family couldn't move past the moment of revelation. He saw the questions in their eyes they were too polite to ask a stranger. He was the one who cross-examined people, not vice versa.

When Juan pressed Ciara for a date, Bryce wanted to smash the other man's face. Bryce wanted the Steele case finished so he could find out the truth about Ciara. He hated feeling desire for a women he thought a spy, a liar, and a betrayer.

He stood apart while Ciara's family hugged her good-bye. Her mother looked with exasperation between Ciara and Juan.

"Juan is a good match for a woman your age," Mrs. Alafita said loud enough so Bryce overheard.

"Mama, I wish you'd stop inviting men over when I'm here. It makes me uncomfortable."

"You force me to do it, *m'hija*. You will not look for a husband on your own."

"You know why I won't, Mama."

"You are still angry. Your brothers and sister married. They are not angry."

"Maybe they were extremely lucky to find people who believe in fidelity. Or maybe they don't care. I do."

"Maybe if you forgave your papa you wouldn't be so angry."

"Don't you dare speak to me about that," Ciara hissed.

What the hell? Every fine-tuned sense of Bryce's went on alert. He took a step forward. Ciara seemed to realize she and her mother had been overheard. She drew herself up and two spots of color blazed in her sculpted cheeks.

"Thank you for inviting me, Mama."

"He's still your papa, Ciara." Her mother's face looked strained.

Ciara's sister and brother-in-law put their arms around Mrs. Alafita and turned her back into the yard. The undercurrents in this family were strong. From what Bryce had overheard, it had something to do with Ciara's father and her relationship with him. She'd lied about wanting to be with her family. She was angry with her parents and somewhat uncomfortable at family gatherings.

Ciara would have to be a cold, heartless bitch and a great actress to hide her true nature from Bryce. But he'd been fooled before. He saw facile liars in his line of work all the time.

He clenched his fists. When this Steele situation was resolved—if he survived—he was getting out of this life. Maybe he'd take a long sabbatical someplace far away to cleanse the filth from his soul.

Ciara strode past him towards her car. She hid her secrets well. Most men wouldn't look past the beautiful package, the lush lying lips.

But he wasn't most men.

CHAPTER 10

"You lied about your family," Bryce accused after he closed his study door so Agent Andrews wouldn't hear.

Ciara jerked and looked guilty. She swallowed. "I didn't lie."

"Yes you did. You said you missed them and wanted to be closer to them. But I thought you and your mother were going to come to blows before we left."

"Families are complicated, you know that."

"No, I don't. You were very angry. I want to know what's going on."

"It's personal. You said you didn't want to discuss personal matters at work."

"Then you shouldn't have taken me to a family function. I'm making it my business because you lied about it."

Ciara wandered to his study window. It was several moments before she spoke. "My father is a philanderer."

It was the last thing Bryce expected to hear. He felt poleaxed.

"I don't know if he was ever faithful to my mother, but she accepted it as her due." Ciara turned to him. The skin on her face was taut, her color heightened by anger. "She's of that generation of Latin women who were taught to expect their Latin husbands to sleep around." Her words were deeply bitter. "I found out in my late teens and it sickened me. But when I told her, she wasn't surprised. She wasn't even angry. She just accepted it."

Ciara began to pace. "My own father." She spat the last word. "Their marriage was a farce. I couldn't get far enough away from it, so I went away to college. I took a job in the AG's office. If she wouldn't leave him, at least I wouldn't see his infidelities. I thought I'd run far enough."

Bryce braced himself. The hurt throbbed off her.

Ciara crossed her arms across her chest. "His latest whore got pregnant and decided to have the baby. My *brother*." She sneered the word. "My mother cried for weeks when she found out. My father spent time with both his families. I couldn't stand for my mother to be humiliated any longer. I'd been telling her for years to leave him, but she wouldn't. She honored her wedding vows even though he had no idea how to be a husband.

"I told my sister my mother would listen to her if she asked her to leave him. My sister is the perfect daughter in every way that I'm not." Again, a slight bitterness tinged her words. "She was newly married and wildly in love with her husband, but she and her husband begged my mother to come live with them. And she did.

"I filed for her legal separation. But she won't divorce him because it's against her religion."

If ever a witness spoke the truth, it was Ciara. If not, she deserved an Academy Award for that performance. But Bryce's gut said it wasn't a lie. She'd seen an injustice and moved to correct it. But she hadn't been completely successful.

She was angry with both her parents. Bryce sensed her father's actions had colored the way she saw life, the way she felt about relationships, maybe even the way she felt about men.

She was hurt. Bryce wanted to hold her and soothe away her pain. He wanted to show her he understood what she was feeling.

What power did Steele wield over her to make her come so close to the source of her pain? "Yet you came home."

Ciara's eyes widened a fraction. "I told you why."

"You've just told me why you shouldn't have."

Ciara turned back to the window. Whatever she said next would be a lie or a half-truth. "I'm tired of being angry."

Bryce hated the lies. He stepped forward and grabbed Ciara's arm, spinning her to face him. "Tell me the truth."

"I am. I have to deal with this. It's affecting me."

He sensed the evasion in her answer, but couldn't pinpoint its source. His anger surged again. "You're free to make your own choices."

"I'm not."

Did she mean Steele? Bryce gripped her arms and tried to read the truth in the dark pools of her eyes. She was so beautiful, a flame to his ice, so passionate, yet as pessimistic about marriage as he was. If she wasn't Steele's tool, maybe together they could forge their own truth about men and women.

The light scent of strawberries teased his nose. He felt the warmth of her body so close to his, and the strength of her arms under his. His body yearned to be closer.

"Bryce?"

Ciara studied him as he studied her. Did she see the same cynicism in his eyes? Did she see the core of ice inside him? Could he make her understand that she could confide in him?

"My parents didn't love each other either," he admitted in a quiet voice. "Their marriage was sterile, loveless, and cold. Money marrying money is often like that. I don't think they loved me, either."

He released her and waved a hand around the study. "This was their house. I lived here with them for twelve years, yet I felt like they were strangers. I knew my nanny better than I knew them. There wasn't much of a difference when I was shipped off to boarding school. There the people who cared for me were just as impersonal."

"Oh, Bryce, I'm so sorry."

"It's no big deal. Lots of rich kids go to boarding school. I fit in there." He shrugged. "But I wonder if I'm capable of feeling anything anymore. My parents were like plastic people, all surface and no depth. I think they must have molded me like them."

Ciara grabbed his arm. "No, Bryce, that's not true."

"Isn't it? I'd like to test that theory."

He took her in his arms. She didn't resist. Slowly he lowered his face to hers giving her every opportunity to avoid him. Her eyes widened. Her body stilled. But her lips parted and he felt their warmth as his touched hers. He forgot about the lies she spoke with them. He savored their passion as she responded to him.

His kiss became hard, urgent. She responded with equal urgency. He had to absorb her passion into himself. He'd been frozen for so long, only coming alive in the courtroom. His hands slid around her waist to bring her body flush against his hungry one. And he was starving. He craved her soft, giving flesh. He needed the strong, slender arms that bound him tight. He felt the tremor in her soft body and knew she craved him too. Need was a flame that heated his loins where they pressed against her feminine flesh. He ached to fill her body, to meet with equal thrusts, to meld into one.

He'd glimpsed her passion and yearned to yoke it to him, to reawaken what he used to be before he became jaded. He could lift her bright sundress, open his shorts, and find the connection he craved.

But then what? He still didn't have answers. Steele was between them even now. Making love wouldn't change anything, not when he didn't trust her. Not when she wouldn't tell him the truth.

Bryce broke the kiss and eased from Ciara's arms. Her dark eyes were glazed with passion, her full lips red and moist from his kisses. He fought the urge to take her to the floor and mount her. His cock ached with fullness.

Ciara touched her fingers to her lips, a telling gesture.

"I want to make love with you," he said.

"I . . ."

He saw the interest in her eyes before her gaze dropped to survey the bulge in his shorts. He felt it like a touch. She licked her lips. She wasn't unaffected.

But he read her answer when she looked up again.

"I can't."

He wasn't really surprised. After hearing her family history, he hadn't thought she'd give herself easily. Well, he didn't either, and for similar reasons.

Ciara walked to the door. With her hand on the knob she faced him. "Maybe the answer won't always be no."

Bryce watched her leave, part glad but part regretful she'd said no. If they made love, they'd resolve nothing but their physical discomfort. As much as he wanted that with her, he needed the truth more. How could a woman who abhorred her father's dishonesty practice deceit? The question gnawed at him.

He returned to his desk to work on Steele's case, but Ciara's face kept swimming into his thoughts. The way she'd looked when he'd pulled away—like a woman ready for loving—kept him semi-aroused.

Bryce knew little about love and relationships. He knew he was capable of love because he loved his friends. But that was completely different from what he assumed he should feel for a woman.

Ciara had reminded her mother about why she didn't marry. Ciara was haunted by her parents' example just as Bryce was by his. She would never fulfill her passionate promise until someone unlocked her from the prison of the past. Saving her would be a challenge worthy of him. Could he get her to trust him enough to tell him the truth about Steele?

• • •

Could Ciara get Bryce to trust her with the truth about Steele? She sat in her living room with the TV muted while she mulled over what had happened in his study. If she'd been another woman— one of her father's many bedmates—she could have been Bryce's sexual plaything today and learned the truth in the aftermath. Her lower body clenched with need. She'd felt his hard arousal pressed against her. His long length would fill that empty place inside her.

She'd thought him cold. But he was anything but cold. His lips had fired her passion. His hard body had awakened her need. She was sure making love with him would be an experience unlike any other.

But he'd held back. Somehow he'd sensed her mission. He was trained to read people, to sense lies and dig for the truth. If she wasn't careful, she'd give herself—and Baisden—away. Before that happened she had to unearth Bryce's secrets.

But how? She'd found nothing in Bryce's files, heard nothing while with Bryce, seen neither Steele nor anyone who worked for him. All she'd seen was Bryce and he was not the man she'd thought he was. She couldn't even give Baisden concrete evidence that Bryce was trustworthy. All she had were feelings, and she'd shown the AG her feelings were biased.

How could she kiss Bryce and think about making love with him when she couldn't prove he was honest? She'd resisted men, and sex, for years. Now all she wanted was to go back to Bryce so they could finish what they'd started.

Ciara had to get herself under control and find Baisden's proof—one way or the other—as soon as possible so she could get back to her life in Lansing. Odd how the thought of leaving Bryce caused a pain in her chest.

Her cell phone rang and she grabbed it off the coffee table, glad to interrupt her painful thoughts. "Hello?"

"It's Carmen. Papa called and Mama answered."

Ciara's muscles tensed to the point of pain. She sat up straight. "What did he want?"

"As soon as I realized it was him, I got on the other phone. He wants her back, of course. He says he misses her enchiladas."

Anger burned in Ciara's veins. She stood and paced the room. "The bastard. His woman probably caught him cheating on her and threw him out."

"He played the Latin card, how a wife's place is with her husband, how she's making him look bad."

"He made himself look bad."

"He made her cry. She's so lonely, Ciara."

Ciara closed her eyes and rubbed her forehead. "She wouldn't be lonely if she divorced him. She could try to find a man who'd love her and treat her right."

"I know. Esteban has an uncle. When he sees Mama he gets tongue-tied. But he respects her wedding vows. Can't you do something, Ciara?"

"Carmen, Mama won't listen to me about divorce. Maybe if you and Esteban broached the subject?"

"I don't know. I'll talk to Esteban about it. Ciara, I can't help remembering how much Papa loved me when I was a little girl."

Ciara barely remembered the golden days before she learned the truth—her father tossing her in the air when she was a child while she squealed with joy, her father calling her his little princess, her father teaching her to ride a bike. The memories hurt with his betrayal.

"And?" she prompted.

"He's good with my children," Carmen said. "They love their visits with him. I think I still love him, despite what he's done to Mama. Is that so wrong?"

Ciara wanted to rant that yes, it was wrong to love a man who hurt you, who hurt other people you loved. It was wrong to love a man who broke your heart and shattered all your little-girl dreams of a perfect papa.

It was wrong for her father to shower his children and grandchildren with affection, but not his own wife. But Carmen wasn't angry with him like Ciara was. Her sister's ideals had held firm until a few years ago.

"I don't know, Carmen," Ciara finally responded to her sister's question.

"Oh." Carmen was silent a moment. "Will you talk to Papa? Tell him to stop calling Mama. I can't do it."

Ciara sighed. "Yes, I'll call him."

"Thanks, Ciara." Her sister disconnected.

Ciara braced herself to make the call, striving for professional detachment. But when her father answered, she was swamped by the hurt she'd felt since she was a teenager.

"Papa."

"Ciara?"

"Yes. Papa, you know you're not supposed to call Mama. You're separated."

"Not by her choice. Or mine." His disapproval and anger seethed through the phone. He knew she was the one who'd initiated her parents' separation.

"She signed the papers, Papa," Ciara reminded him.

"You made her. And now she has changed her mind and you will not let her end the separation like she wants to. She wants to come home. I want her to come home."

"To a bed where your whore is currently sleeping."

"Ashley is not a whore. She is your youngest brother's mother. A brother you have never met, I remind you."

How dare he scold her about familial duty. "He's living proof that my father is an adulterer."

"I am a man, Ciara. I have needs. I do not expect you to understand."

"What you have is no self-control. You don't know how to honor vows."

"I am not going to argue Latin marriage with you," he said, his voice stiff.

Ciara felt unclean. "No, you're not. If you can't honor the separation contract, like you can't honor wedding vows, we'll get a restraining order against you."

"Ciara, you cannot do that. She is my wife!" he shouted.

"You went into the marriage in bad faith. That's an argument for annulment in the church's eyes."

"No, that is a lie."

"You never intended to honor your vows. It's time you let Mama have a divorce."

"She does not want a divorce, and neither do I. I want my wife back and there is nothing you can do to stop her from coming home where she belongs."

Ciara felt cold all the way through. "And where would your precious Ashley go?"

"Ashley knows I am married. She knew this time was only temporary, until Ascension returned home. I will get her an apartment, or a house."

"And your son?"

"He is mine. A son should live with his father. I will talk to your mother about something called shared parenting with Ashley."

CHAPTER 11

Shared parenting. Ciara hung up before her volcanic rage at her father escaped her lips. Anger drove her to her feet to pace the confines of her hotel room. It was hideous to imagine her mother cooking for her father's bastard, forced to take care of the child during the day while her father was at work, forced to face her husband's infidelity twenty-four seven. My God, Ciara couldn't believe her father's audacity.

Ciara didn't understand why her mother had married him. And that she wanted to go back to him. She was as bad as the women who stayed with physical abusers. Ciara would never allow herself to be cheated on and lied to and humiliated like her mother had. How could she stop her mother from going back for more?

But when Ciara's anger died, doubt crept in. Didn't her mother have the right to make bad choices? Freedom meant having free will. Ciara just didn't know where free will crossed the line to self-destruction. At what point could family members intervene? What Ciara wanted for her mother wasn't so wrong, but velvet chains were still chains. Was Ciara hurting her mother with her righteous opinions?

Ciara had no answers. She felt too strongly about this issue to be unbiased. She'd have to tell her mother this new development face to face. She called Carmen to warn her she was coming over.

By the time she'd driven to Royal Oak, her back and shoulder muscles were knotted with tension. An unsmiling Carmen answered the door and led her to their mother. Her mother took one look at Ciara and her face crumpled.

Ciara knelt at her mother's feet and took hold of her mother's cold hands. "Carmen, please send the children away, but you and Esteban need to hear this."

As her mother sobbed quietly, Carmen shooed the children upstairs. Then she returned to sit on the couch holding Esteban's hand.

Ciara repeated the conversation with her father. Carmen gasped when Ciara reported her father's plan.

Her mother's face was lined with strain. "But he cannot believe I would want her child in my house."

"He does, Mama. You've accepted his cheating. Why not the result of his affair?"

But her mother shook her head in negation. "You are painting him as a bad man. You did not repeat his words correctly. He would not ask this of me."

Ciara stiffened, overly sensitive to being called a liar at the moment. "I repeated everything he said. All I left out was my bad behavior."

"But no man asks this of his wife, not in America."

"Mama," Carmen scolded. "No man asks his wife to turn a blind eye while he sleeps around. Esteban would never ask it of me. Besides, I wouldn't put up with that and he knows it. I couldn't ask for a more faithful husband."

Shock reverberated through Ciara. She'd wondered about her sister's marriage but had been afraid to ask, afraid to know the truth. Ciara felt dizzy with unexpected hope. She'd thought all men were untrustworthy liars. But if her brother-in-law could be trusted, maybe other men could be as well?

Her mother's lip quivered. She studied her son-in-law.

"I would never do such a thing to Carmen," Esteban assured her. "Or to my family."

"And Papa flaunts his infidelity," Carmen continued, "Not just for you to see, but for me and my children, for Carlos Junior and

Francisco's children to see. Papa has shamed us all. An honorable man would set you free."

Their mother gasped. "Divorce?"

"You deserve to be appreciated as Esteban values me. As I cherish and respect him. I don't want to see you treated this way anymore. Divorce would give you a fresh start, another chance, perhaps a man who'll honor you."

Mrs. Alafita shook her head. "Divorce is wrong."

"So is adultery, Mama. The Ten Commandments don't list divorce, but they do list adultery."

"But I will be alone," their mother wailed.

Esteban slid off the couch and knelt by Ciara's side. "You're welcome in our home for as long as you wish to live here. I know Carmen is glad you're here. The children love you."

"And I love them. But divorce . . . "

Carmen knelt beside her husband. "A beginning, Mama, not an ending."

"If you want to go back to Papa, we can't stop you," Ciara said.

Carmen's gaze jerked to her and she gasped, "No."

"But you know what you face," Ciara added.

Her mother's eyes were dark with misery. "You are telling the truth?"

"Yes, Mama," Ciara answered.

Her mother sobbed. "I cannot go back to that. I will not." She gripped her hands together in her lap.

Ciara gave her mother a few moments to cry and wipe her eyes with a tissue. Then she asked, "What do you want me to do?"

Carmen and Esteban laid their hands on her mother's. "We love you, Mama. We want you to be happy."

Mrs. Alafita looked at Esteban. "You believe my husband is wrong? That he has dishonored me?"

Esteban nodded. "Yes, Mama. A man cherishes his wife and honors her above all others. My father taught me that."

Her mother turned to Ciara. She drew a shuddering breath. "Draw up the papers. I will sign them. I will not let him do this to me."

Ciara bowed her head. "Yes, Mama."

Carmen and Esteban rose to place their arms around Ciara's mother. Ciara moved out of their way, surreptitiously wiping a tear from her cheek. Her mother had chosen. It was what Ciara had wanted for years, so why did her chest feel so tight? Why was there no sense of victory in this decision?

"It's best for you, Mama," Esteban rumbled. "You've lived in limbo a long time."

"We all have, Mama," Carmen agreed.

Ciara agreed too. Now they could all move forward, including her. She hoped.

CHAPTER 12

"We have a meeting with Adam Steele at ten," Bryce greeted Ciara first thing the next morning.

Ciara tamped down her excitement. Here was the break she'd wanted. "He must be anxious if he's called already."

"He called me at home yesterday." Bryce was at his most inscrutable.

Ciara frowned. "Then why didn't you give him a status update yesterday?" Damn, they'd probably handled the private stuff already.

"Mr. Steele prefers to discuss the case in person."

Lucky for her. "I'll gather all the files." She turned to leave.

Bryce's voice halted her. "Ciara."

She turned back. "Do you need something?"

The heat in Bryce's blue eyes caused a melting sensation in her lower abdomen.

"Will you go out with me tomorrow night?"

Ciara could barely breathe. Her heart pounded with excitement. "Out? On a date?"

"There's a Bar Association mixer at the Highland Meadows Country Club. It's a dinner/dance. I think I can handle the slow dances."

Slow dancing with Bryce. On a date. Ciara swallowed. "Are you sure you want to go out with me?"

"Definitely."

"Then, sure, I'll go. I love to dance."

"You said maybe the answer wouldn't always be no."

Ciara couldn't speak. Her breath stalled in her throat. Did he think the answer would be yes on Friday? If he asked, would she say no? He looked wonderful in his navy pinstriped suit with the power red tie. Confident, successful, in control. She'd like to place herself in his sure hands and let him do whatever he liked with her. Her face heated, her heart rate galloped, and she fled without answering.

She'd worked with successful men before, but never mixed sex with business, not that she was now. She felt off balance with Bryce, as though she weren't sure which world she should be in: the personal or the professional.

When she returned with the files, Bryce looked up and speared her with a glance. "Have I made you uncomfortable?"

"A little," she admitted.

"Good. I don't want to be the only one."

Her body felt overheated, her knit dress too tight. Their eyes locked. She felt like she was falling into their cerulean depths. His eyes were heated, yet cool—as fickle as her body's temperature. She moistened her lips remembering yesterday's kiss. Her gaze dropped to his firm lips. She wanted to taste them again.

Bryce made no move, but waited, his vaunted control giving him the appearance of cool and calm. How could he not tremble with the memory of the fire they'd created as they pressed together? How could his breathing be so calm when she felt like her chest heaved with heavy panting? She could smell his light cologne, released from his body heat. She wanted to touch his body too, run her hands up the hard planes of his chest. She wanted to wrinkle his blindingly white shirt that shouted control. She wanted to muss his perfect hair.

She wanted to get messy with him. She wanted him out of control. She felt like throwing herself at him to break his icy coolness.

His hand twitched. She exhaled, knowing he was barely holding onto his composure. She wouldn't push him to snap. She wasn't ready for the consequences.

As she walked out of his office, she turned and caught him exhaling. A smile of pure pleasure teased her lips.

Down the hall in the cubicle she'd been assigned, Ciara felt like she was on pins and needles. Her body still reacted to the encounter with Bryce and now she had nearly two hours to await Adam Steele. She should be wearing a wire; otherwise, anything she heard could be hearsay evidence. She should have brought a tape recorder to work, although she had no place to hide it.

She should be interviewing witnesses for the State, doing her best to make the case iron clad. Because lying to Bryce was one thing, but lying to a mobster could be fatal. But it was too late to change course now. She was on point. It was up to her. She hoped her true feelings for Steele didn't show on her face.

The intercom startled her from her research. "Ciara, Mr. Steele is here. Please come to my office," Bryce ordered.

"I'll be right there." Ciara headed down the hall with her notebook. She'd see the mobster up close for the first time.

She passed a very large man in a black suit outside Bryce's door. His dark eyes were cold and soulless. Steele must have brought a bodyguard.

Ciara entered Bryce's office and had eyes only for Steele. Graying, fifty-three, of medium build, in a charcoal pinstriped suit, Steele resembled an elegant gentleman. Belatedly she realized he was sizing her up, but not as a man would an attractive female. It was only as his dead gray eyes met hers that she understood he was doing a threat assessment. What he'd decided, however, she couldn't tell.

"Mr. Steele, this is my new assistant Ciara Alafita. Ciara, Adam Steele."

Ciara shook Steele's hand. Never in a thousand years would she have believed she'd do such a thing. She worked in the AG's office to help people however she could. Steele and his ilk were the AG's enemy. But this close to him she felt vulnerable. She was glad he didn't know the real reason she was here.

• • •

Bryce watched Ciara and Steele. There was no hint of recognition or familiarity on either's part, but then Ciara had probably been coached on how to act around the man who controlled her. Bryce had foolishly hoped they would give away their real relationship.

One thing he thought he could say for certain: Ciara and Steele weren't lovers. Bryce felt savage satisfaction over that. Those two could still be the greatest actors in the world, but his gut said on this issue he wasn't wrong.

Ciara sat in the second visitor's chair next to Steele.

"How's my defense coming along?" Steele asked as soon as he was seated.

"I'm going through the Grand Jury indictment piece by piece to dispute each item," Bryce explained. "I have Miss Alafita re-interviewing witnesses. We've researched relevant cases and appeals—"

"Give me specifics," Steele demanded.

"I believe we've discredited the witness for one count of extortion. He has no first-hand knowledge of a crime. Without his testimony, his physical evidence is inadmissible."

"Good. What else?"

"We haven't been able to interview all the witnesses yet. It's our top priority. As you know, there have been some . . . obstacles."

"Yes, I heard the security in this office was breached for the second time. You appear unharmed."

Bryce wondered if anyone besides Ciara had told him. "I'm fine, but diagnostic tests took most of the day."

"Dr. Khalil needs his own equipment in his office."

Bryce controlled his jolt of surprise. But he should have realized Steele would know his doctor's name. "I came through the ER, not Dr. Khalil's office. He was required to use their facilities until I was released."

"These security breaches concern me. A larger bomb could have a devastating effect on my case. I'd like to loan you one of my private security guards."

Bryce held very still. Steele had no way of knowing who around him was disloyal. But Bryce couldn't let on he knew, not with Ciara in the room.

"That's very gracious of you, Mr. Steele, but not necessary."

"I insist. My freedom is at stake."

Steele had to know about the Feds. Ciara told him everything. What was he trying to do, get his own man inside federal protection? Steele already had Ciara here.

"My office manager is stopping packages at the door now. Anything even remotely questionable earns a call to the bomb squad. The bomber won't get to me again."

"What about at home? That Mercedes was a classic."

Of course Steele knew about that too. Bryce was cornered, right where Steele wanted him. "Mr. Steele, you know I already have protection."

Steele steepled his hands in front of him. "It seems a conflict of interest to me to involve the FBI." His eyes were glacial.

Bryce's chest tightened. So the local FBI was compromised. He wondered how badly his safety was compromised. "I assure you there's no conflict."

"They work for the very government prosecuting me. I don't want them near my case. I wonder why you felt you needed them."

Bryce found he had a white-knuckled grip on his pen. It was an order, plain and simple, with Steele's doubt out in the open. If Steele were sure Bryce was working with the FBI, he'd be dead within a day. However, there was no guarantee he'd survive Steele's security anyway.

So this was why Adam Steele had made a personal visit. "You're my client," Bryce temporized. "I'd never presume to borrow anything from you, including personnel."

"Now we've cleared up that misunderstanding. My security will replace the FBI within the hour." Steele rose.

Bryce tried to limit his risk. "You'll handpick someone?" He spoke with an off-handed confidence he didn't feel.

Steele pierced him with an arctic stare. Bryce wouldn't back down on this. "All my security is handpicked."

Bryce didn't know if that was a yes or not. "Don't you want to discuss your defense?"

"I pay you to handle that. I know you'll get me acquitted. I'll see you in court on Monday." Steele walked out the door.

Bryce slowly unclenched his muscles. He glanced at Ciara. She was looking at the doorway.

She turned back to him. "Why did you let him replace the FBI?"

"Why do you think I did?"

"He threatened you. You could tell the FBI."

"How long do you think I'd live if I refused his offer?"

"So you caved."

"There is no safety in this for me. Instead of sure death, I get to play Russian roulette with my life."

"Because of Steele's rival."

Bryce nodded. "Let's get the rest of the witnesses interviewed. We need to dispute the racketeering charges."

Ciara looked like she wanted to say something more, but she rose and strode out the door. That black knit dress did killer things for her figure—the proud thrust of her breasts, her firm tush and those long, long legs. Too bad he didn't have time to savor her, but the clock was ticking on this case and possibly on his life.

He called Agent Pollack. "It's Bryce Gannon. I don't need protection anymore. You can withdraw your agent."

"What's happened? I haven't heard the local cops caught the bomber."

"No, they didn't. I've got private security now."

"I don't understand. Why didn't you pay for a bodyguard before?"

"It didn't occur to me."

"But it has now."

"I appreciate what you've done for me."

"Just doing our job. What made you think of a bodyguard now anyway?"

Ah, Pollack was suspicious. "Somebody in your office was bound to squeal to Steele."

"Thanks a lot, Gannon."

Within the hour a man in his early thirties presented himself in Bryce's office. He was lean and moved like a big cat. In his eyes was death.

"Compliments of Mr. Steele. I'm Durayev." With his sandy blonde hair he could have been an all-American man. Except for the brown eyes that were cold like the dirt on a winter grave.

"Have you been with Mr. Steele long?" Bryce asked.

"Seven years."

Maybe Steele had handpicked this man. "I'll probably be here in my office all day."

"I'll be around."

Minutes later Pollack called. "What the hell are you playing at, Gannon? Agent West said Adam Steele showed up and then you called me to pull the detail. It's his security, isn't it?"

"It's interesting how much of what *you* do is common knowledge," Bryce hinted to the agent.

There was a telling silence. "Are you saying we have a leak?"

"I hope my new security reports only to me."

"I hope your new security reports only to Steele," Pollack said. "You're taking a big risk."

"I'd say the odds were fifty-fifty. Are yours better or worse?"

"Bastard. I hope you survive this thing."

"Me too."

Pollack's tone changed. "You need anything?"

"Will a flak jacket protect me from a bullet to the head?"

"No." Pollack actually sounded sympathetic.

"Then I guess I don't need anything. Thanks, Agent Pollack."

"Call if you change your mind."

"I won't."

After Bryce hung up, he felt abandoned. Now there was just him and the professional killer, who might or might not plan to kill him.

Oh, and Steele's beautiful spy.

CHAPTER 13

"The case against Adam Stele is falling apart," Ciara told Baisden when she reported in later that afternoon. She sat in her car with the windows rolled down to let the summer heat escape.

"Witnesses are recanting. One left town without a forwarding address. I interviewed one witness myself who has no first-hand knowledge of Steele's racketeering activities. With Bryce's track record he might be able to get Steele acquitted if the government fails to prove at least two counts."

"Ciara, you know in any case against an alleged mobster witnesses will become afraid of testifying the closer the court date gets. And I'm sure Steele is threatening the witnesses."

Her free hand fisted. "It's not right that I'm helping ruin the government's case."

"You think Gannon would leave any stone unturned if you weren't there?"

"No, but I doubt he'd have covered as much ground as I have as quickly as I have. He's not operating at a hundred percent. If it was just him, he'd be scrambling right up to court next week."

"Ciara, be realistic. Gannon would have used his staff to do the legwork you're doing. He's the show, not a roadie."

"I'm better than his staff," she argued.

"That may be true, but he still would have gotten the interviews. The U.S. Attorney should have built a better case."

"I met Adam Steele today." Ciara told Baisden all about the visit.

"So you witnessed no illegal activity."

She took a swallow of her bottled water. "No. My presence might have restrained both men."

"It was worth a try. Keep your ears open. Have you finished your assessment of Gannon yet?"

"No. He keeps his secrets to himself. And after the confrontation with Steele over security I'm not sure about their relationship. They're both cold, calculating men. It was like watching the clash of the Titans, even though Steele is more powerful."

"Do you believe Gannon is in danger?"

Ciara sighed. "Yes. But I don't think we can do anything about it."

"Then be careful. I don't want you caught in the crossfire."

Ciara agreed. "Will do."

"Only a few more days until the trial starts."

If Bryce survived.

"And then you can come home. You've done well so far, Ciara."

But after she hung up, she felt like she was failing everyone—the people, the AG, her family . . . and Bryce. When had she begun to feel she and Bryce were a team? He challenged her on a professional and personal level, yet she felt equal to him. She'd never felt that way before. It was a good thing she'd be going back home soon.

She had to tell Bryce what she'd learned. After calling to make sure he hadn't left the office, she fought freeway traffic to get there. The closer she got, the more nerves fluttered in her stomach.

The first thing she saw when she entered the lobby was the man with the light brown hair. He looked up when she opened the door and speared her with a quick head-to-toe assessment. That alone would have set off all her internal alarms, but his arctic, dead eyes had her wanting to run for safety.

Ciara glanced at the receptionist.

"Welcome back, Ciara," the young woman piped in a too-bright voice.

Ciara noted the man stopped staring at her. This had to be Steele's security.

She halted at the reception desk. "Any messages, Aimee?"

"No."

Ciara lowered her voice, although she wondered if the man had acute hearing. "Who is that?"

"Mr. Steele sent him to protect Mr. Gannon. He makes me nervous." Aimee darted a quick glance at the man.

He made Ciara nervous too. "Just keep in mind that as long as he's here, Mr. Gannon is safe." She hoped.

"I'm trying."

Ciara walked down the hall to Bryce's office and knocked on the doorframe.

Bryce looked up from his stacks of books and papers and signaled her in. He'd taken off his suit jacket, leaving him in his bright white shirt. She could see the inhaler in his pocket and was surprised he'd let it show at work.

"You were gone a long time." He didn't hide the question implied in the statement.

Ciara set her briefcase in a chair and pulled out papers. "I saw four witnesses and spent several hours trying to track down several more. One skipped town." She sorted the papers and handed him the witness's dossier. "His landlord said he moved out. His employer said he quit."

Bryce looked at the paper and jotted notes on his legal pad.

"These two witnesses recanted." She handed him the pages.

"Recanted?" His golden brows lifted.

"Yes. They didn't witness any illegal activity and they don't want to testify.

"Here are the other statements. I'm afraid those witnesses confirmed their earlier depositions." She handed those to him.

"But we're in better shape than we were this morning."

"I thought you'd be pleased."

"I am. Good work. If you plan to stay late, I'll order in something for us to eat."

"Thanks, Bryce, but I can't stay tonight. I have something personal I need to do." She had the divorce papers in her briefcase.

"Oh, that's okay."

"Did you need me to work late?"

"No. I would have been happy for the company."

A little thrill ran through her. "I wish I could. I could take some things home with me and work on them later."

"No. I don't want the case spread out in too many places."

She didn't think he'd told her the truth, but she didn't know why he'd lie about it either. "Then I'll see you tomorrow morning. You should go home to work. That way you can relax a little."

"I'm perfectly comfortable here."

"It won't be long until it's just you and Steele's security in the office. How comfortable will you be then?"

"If he's going to kill me, he won't care where."

"Then if you turn up dead tomorrow, we'll know who did it."

"Steele's hit man. What a perfect setup to take Steele down."

"You should have stuck with the Feds."

"I couldn't. You know that better than anyone."

Ciara didn't want Bryce dead, but no argument of hers would sway him. This fatalism seemed out of character to the man who'd cheated death and worked from his hospital bed. She knew some people suffered depression after a near-fatal trauma. Maybe that was Bryce's case.

She studied him. He didn't seem depressed. He studied her in return, calm and detached, in control of his domain. No, she didn't have to worry about that with him.

"Did you find what you were looking for?" he asked.

"I think so."

His lips quirked in a smile. "Good. Save that thought for tomorrow night's dancing."

Unable to speak as awareness prickled her skin and sped her pulse rate, Ciara nodded and escaped.

• • •

When she left, Ciara drained the light from the room and Bryce felt let down. Since this morning he'd been looking forward to sharing dinner with her. Damn, what sort of personal life did she have in town? Did she have a date with the man from the picnic after all? Bryce's hands fisted around his pencil.

He was sure if it had been a family thing Ciara would have said so. Was she meeting Steele? God, he couldn't stand the thought of the two of them together. His muscles tightened in protest and the pencil snapped.

Bryce threw the pieces away and thought about the case instead. He'd expected witnesses to recant. But with the discredited testimony and the witness skipping town, as Ciara said, Steele's case was looking like a winner. Bryce couldn't let that happen. If Steele were set free, he'd haunt Bryce's life forever.

Ciara would report Bryce's successful movements and thus keep Steele from sensing Bryce's true intentions until too late. He only needed some privacy to find the answers, and to survive until the trial.

After his staff left, Bryce packed up his briefcase and sought out Durayev. "I'm heading home."

"I'll make sure the way is clear."

Bryce waited while his bodyguard checked the hall, then he locked the office and set the security system. Durayev walked him to his car, where the bodyguard dropped to his knee and checked under Bryce's rented Audi sedan. Bryce's neck and back itched, like he had a big target painted on him. He wiped clammy palms on his slacks. He glanced around, but saw no snipers and no mad bombers. Damn, he hated this.

Durayev rose and dusted his hands. "All clear. I'll follow you."

"Do you know the address if we get separated?"

"Don't worry about that." Durayev's expression was inscrutable, so Bryce didn't ask further questions.

Ciara was right about home being more relaxing than the office. Mrs. McCleary had left chicken Kiev and a salad in the fridge. Durayev ate quickly without saying a word and returned to prowling the house. Bryce finished his delicious meal in lonely silence. He hadn't been lonely in years, not since he'd met Paul, Roger, and Sean. He didn't know what had altered in the past few weeks, but something had.

He changed into casual clothes and worked for several hours in his study poring over the evidence looking for some fact he could overlook without Ciara catching it, or some seemingly innocuous piece of evidence that was, in fact, damning. He found plenty that would help the State win its case if he could lose openly. But nothing he could hide from Ciara. She was too good a lawyer. Steele had chosen her well. Bryce could not do anything that Ciara would call to Steele's attention.

When the doorbell rang, Bryce was ready for a break. His temples throbbed from the strain.

A few moments later, Durayev appeared in the study doorway. "Christian and Gabrielle Ziko are here. I wanted to make sure I should let them in."

Bryce was surprised the younger Zikos were here. "Of course." He followed Durayev to the door.

Gabrielle hugged Bryce a little too long. He tried not to stiffen knowing she was psychically reading him.

When she released him, she looked from him to Durayev with a frown.

"Come in and sit down," Bryce said, to stop her from saying anything in front of the bodyguard.

Christian and Gabrielle settled on the couch in the living room, pressed together from shoulder to knee. Bryce felt a pang of jealousy over the way they seemed to be halves of a whole.

"You're feeling all right?" Christian asked.

"Fine," Bryce replied.

"Then why is that man here?" Gabrielle demanded.

"He's security."

"He's not a cop or a Fed."

"Leave it be, Gabrielle."

Christian took hold of Gabrielle's hand and they shared a deep look. Bryce felt shut out even though he knew he would never share with a woman what the two of them shared. He wasn't psychic. He'd never wanted to be . . . until now. Until he watched them share a bond so deep no one else could touch it. He'd lived with superficial romantic relationships for too long. Now he wanted someone tuned into his thoughts and his moods in the normal way of people who deeply loved one another, and he wanted to tune into a woman in the same way. It was something his parents hadn't had, but which Paul Ziko and his wife had shared early in their marriage, and which Christian and Gabrielle shared in spades.

"You're risking everything, Bryce," Gabrielle said when she faced him again.

The hair on the back of Bryce's neck stood on end. He didn't ask Gabrielle how she knew.

"Some things are worth the risk. You and Christian should understand." Bryce glanced toward the doorway. The couple followed his gaze. Gabrielle's eyes widened.

They shared another look and then Christian squeezed Gabrielle's hand. "We wanted you to know we're going to have a baby."

Bryce took the news like a kick in the gut. The couple in front of him blurred unexpectedly and his breath came hard. He might be dead by next week, but the people around him were finding happiness and going forward with their lives and long-range plans.

"Congratulations," he managed. As his breaths got shorter, he tried to circumvent the oncoming asthma-like attack.

Their blinding, delighted smiles made him feel even smaller and meaner for envying them their joy. They deserved this happiness.

As their excitement bubbled over, Bryce calmed the attack by degrees until he was breathing normally again. He was master of his health, not the ricin damage. Slowly he was able to warm to the younger Zikos' bliss.

"You'll be an honorary uncle, of course," Gabrielle explained.

"Of course." But Bryce realized he'd rather be a father and hold his own child. He'd rather help mold a son or daughter into a better person than he'd become. He'd like a second chance to be a human, to experience love first-hand, and to return love unstintingly. But time might run out before he could grab another chance to do more with his life.

A picture of Ciara filled his mind as she held one of her nieces. Ciara knew how to love family. She knew how to love period. Whatever reason she was Steele's tool didn't strip her humanity from her. She'd been hurt by life like he had. Like him, she was particular about whom she loved. Maybe together . . . The thought tantalized. If he could find out why she spied for Steele.

"Our son will be born shortly after New Year's." Gabrielle looked like the Madonna as she spoke, an appropriate likeness for the occasion.

"You know you're having a boy?" Bryce asked.

"Gabrielle saw it in a vision," Christian said.

Bryce was sorely tempted to ask Gabrielle to try to read his future. She'd told him she had no control over her gift and she rarely predicted what had yet to happen, but it was worth a try. However, if he had no future, he didn't want to know.

CHAPTER 14

Ciara laid the divorce papers gently in her mother's hands. Ciara knew it was like handing her mother a bomb—the divorce was going to explode and destroy her mother's life, as she knew it. Ciara, her sister, and her brother-in-law hoped her mother could rebuild a better life from the rubble.

"So light," her mother said staring at the papers. "So few pages."

Ciara glanced at Carmen and Esteban. "Divorce is easy now, Mama."

"Carlos will get a copy?" Mrs. Alafita asked.

"I'll file the signed papers with the court tomorrow. Papa will be served papers next week."

"By a stranger. By surprise."

"Yes. That's how it's done."

"He should be told beforehand." Her mother's dark eyes pleaded with Ciara's.

"You want to tell him?" In her peripheral vision Ciara saw her sister adamantly shaking her head.

"He'll try to change your mind," Ciara said.

"I know he was wrong, now. Esteban has shown me how an honorable man treats a wife. Carlos will not change my mind."

Ciara's chest felt tight. Not all men were cheating bastards wanting something better than what they had. She understood that now and was trying to accept it.

"Do you want one of us on the extension with you?" she asked.

"You are my lawyer, Ciara."

"Papa and I are barely civil to one another."

"You can be civil, for me."

Ciara nodded acceptance. "Yes, Mama."

The three women sat on the couch with Ciara's mother in the middle and both cordless phones. Esteban sat on the carpet at Carmen's feet holding his mother-in-law's free hand.

Her father answered on the second ring sounding slightly out of breath. A small child giggled close to the receiver.

"Hello?"

"Carlos," Mrs. Alafita breathed.

"Ascension! My darling! Wait a minute." There was hushed conversation and the giggling moved away from the phone and then stopped. "Ascension, have you called to say you are coming home?" Mrs. Alafita stiffened like a board. "You know it is not right for us to live apart like this. The church frowns on it."

"And God frowns on adultery, Carlos. No, I am not coming back to you. Ever. I called to tell you I am divorcing you."

"No! Ascension, Ciara has poisoned your mind. We had a good marriage. I was a good provider to you and our children. Nearly thirty-two years I loved you, took care of you, gave you a home, children, grandchildren. You had everything a woman could want."

A tear rolled down Mrs. Alafita's cheek. "Not faithfulness, Carlos."

"I am a Latin man. My passions run hot. You cannot expect me to sate myself on my wife. That is not what a wife is for."

"Yes, I can expect it. And I should have. I was wrong to put up with it. You will receive divorce papers next week."

"Ascension, you cannot do this to me. It is wrong. Please, if you will see me, you will change your mind. I will come over now."

"No!" her mother said a little sharply. "No, we will not talk about this. I have decided."

"This is Ciara's doing! She has poisoned you against me with her man hating. I do not know how I raised such a daughter."

Ciara's body heated with anger, but still she tried to hold back her angry remark.

But to her surprise, her mother responded, "Daughters should think their father is a hero, a man of perfect valor and honor. Carmen and Ciara could not think of you that way, Carlos."

Ciara's father sputtered, but her mother wasn't done. "And if my sons treat their wives as dishonorably as you treated me, I will bear the shame to my grave. I am lucky Carmen has found a man who honors God and his wife." Esteban squeezed her hand.

"Thank you for my children, Carlos."

"Ascension, you cannot divorce me!" Ciara's father sounded desperate. "I need you."

"But I no longer need you," Mrs. Alafita disconnected. She looked at her daughters and Esteban. "He will never change."

"No, Mama, he won't," Carmen agreed.

"I do not want my sons to be like him." Tears filled her mother's dark eyes.

"Talk to them, Mama," Esteban urged. "I'll talk to them too if there's need."

"I will call them tonight to arrange to see them. I want to see their faces when they talk to me."

When it was time to leave, her mother walked Ciara to the door. Mrs. Alafita shooed Carmen and Esteban away.

"What your father said about you . . . " her mother picked her words carefully.

Ciara's cheeks burned with shame. "It's true, Mama. Even my old boss knew I was angry at men."

Her mother took hold of her hands. "This is more of my shame, that you feel this way about men because of me."

"No, Mama!"

"We will speak truth, Ciara. I think there have been enough lies in our family. You are angry with me too for letting it happen."

Ciara blew out a breath. "Yes."

"I will work for your forgiveness. If you will help me, I will learn to listen to my daughter's wisdom."

"Mama, I never wanted to hurt you. I wanted *him* to stop hurting you."

"I understand that now. I was a fool about so many things." Her mother began to cry.

Ciara enfolded her mother in her arms and cried with her. Slowly the tightness in her chest eased. There would be dark days in her mother's near future, but there would be dawn. Could Ciara be as brave as her mother and change her view of men? Could there be a dawn for her too?

• • •

"Did you finish your personal business last night?" Bryce asked Ciara as he drove the rented Audi to the Bar Association function the next evening.

It was the first time they'd been alone together all day. She glanced in the back seat where Durayev sat. Well, not alone exactly. Durayev had quite a dampening effect. She swallowed.

"Yes." She'd filed the signed divorce papers with the court today.

"If we didn't have this trial coming up, I'd tell you to take a day off. It can't be easy for you living out of a hotel, searching for a place to live, and tying up loose ends in Lansing."

Guilt ate at her. Her face felt hot. "It's not. But I have my evenings and lunch hours free."

"That makes for long days. You should have refused my invitation for tonight."

"You said there'd be dancing, Bryce. You made a verbal contract with me and I'm holding you to it."

The side of his mouth kicked up in a smile. "Yes, counselor. Do you have any big plans for this weekend?"

Other than laundry and painting her toenails? "Nothing special. You?"

"I'd like to go fishing with my friends, but I doubt it's going to happen. There's a storm predicted for Saturday and I don't want to be out on the lake in one."

"Lake Erie?"

"Yeah. The squalls move in fast and make the lake pretty rough."

She'd never been on a boat or on the lake. It sounded like fun. "How often do you go out?"

"Not often enough." Bryce grimaced. "In fact, I haven't been out at all this year."

"You should make time to relax."

"I know. Do you?"

"I help coach a teen girl's church basketball team. Or I did. There's a game Sunday I'd like to go back for."

Bryce pulled into the country club parking lot and found an empty spot. Other couples were dressed as they were, in suits and pretty dresses, but none of them had brought a bodyguard. Durayev wore a dark suit, so at least he blended in.

Bryce's black suit looked wonderful on him and made his shoulders look impossibly wide. But he was too stark for Ciara's taste—cold blonde hair, stark white shirt and black suit. Even his tie was a subdued black and white. He needed warmth.

Well she certainly made up for his lack. Her scarlet dress with the full, knee-length skirt edged in black lace announced her presence in no uncertain terms.

As she wobbled on the unaccustomed four-inch heels, Bryce took her arm to steady her. An electric thrill ran from his warm hand to her bicep and into her lower abdomen. She caught her breath. In these heels she was the same height as him. She couldn't wait to slow dance with him. She'd probably daydream they were making love instead.

She'd never been to the Highland Meadows Country Club before. Inside they were directed to a room that was floor-to-ceiling glass on two sides. Outside she glimpsed a putting green and manicured lawn sloping down to the golf course. It was an impressive room. The chandelier light sparkled off the china and glassware on the tables.

"Do you have a membership here?" Ciara asked Bryce.

"No. I don't play much golf."

"I'd have thought you'd have a membership somewhere for impressing clients."

"I'm a trial lawyer. My clients aren't the type I have to impress like that."

"Oh." She wondered where he'd met Adam Steele.

Bryce introduced her to dozens of legal professionals. They mingled, exchanged business cards and gossip, and networked. He halted them before a distinguished-looking Hispanic man in his late fifties.

"Gannon," the man held out his hand.

Bryce gripped it. "Judge Garcia. Ciara, this is Judge Andy Garcia. Judge, my new legal assistant Ciara Alafita." They shook hands. "He's presiding over the Steele case," Bryce added.

"I thought I wouldn't see you in my courtroom so soon, if at all," Judge Garcia said.

"Rumors of my death have been greatly exaggerated."

The judge smiled, his teeth white against his swarthy skin. "I'm glad to hear it. You're feeling all right?"

"Yes, sir."

The judge lowered his voice. "The police haven't arrested anyone for the bombing."

"No, sir, they haven't."

"I've asked for security measures, just in case."

"I don't think anyone will attempt something in a crowded courtroom."

"I'm not taking chances." Judge Garcia glanced around. "I have to mingle. I'll see you in court Monday."

"Yes, sir."

The judge moved away to greet other people.

"He seems nice," Ciara said.

"Don't let his social manner fool you. He's a stickler in the courtroom."

She looked him in the eye. "So will he be a detriment to your case?"

"No. I think he'll rule according to the law and the preponderance of evidence."

Here was the perfect opening. "Have you studied judges since you were approached to run as one?"

"I study judges as part of my job. It's like knowing how to win at poker with the hand you've been dealt."

"You mean like bluffing?"

"No. I mean knowing each judge's rules and their strengths and weaknesses. Then I know how to use the hand I have to win."

"Do you want to be a judge?"

"I think so."

Ciara glanced at Durayev, who was searching the crowd. His eyes roved constantly, checking, assessing, classifying. Ciara imagined anyone approaching Bryce got the x-ray vision treatment. She'd bet Durayev could identify clothing bulges and tell her who was packing in this crowd.

She hoped he couldn't hear her. "Adam Steele could help get you elected."

"Yes, he could." It was a flat statement.

"Do you want his help?"

"First I have to get him acquitted."

Someone tapped on a microphone. Ciara looked toward the front of the room where a man at the podium asked people to take their seats. Bryce steered her to their table.

A tall, curvaceous blonde stepped up to them as they reached the table. Ciara would have recognized Bryce's ex-girlfriend anywhere. The woman was gorgeous.

"Bryce, it's wonderful to see you again," Monique said in her perfectly cultivated voice. "I didn't know you'd be here."

"It's good for the case if I'm seen here tonight."

"Of course, the case." She sounded resigned.

"Who are you with?" Bryce asked.

"Pierce Gallaher of Windell, Gallaher, and Crawley."

"Ah."

"And you're here with . . . I'm sorry but I've forgotten your name," Monique said.

"Ciara Alafita," Ciara provided, although she was sure the other woman knew her name. She shook Monique's hand. Monique gave Ciara a cold, cursory once-over.

A man signaled from a few tables over. Monique waved at him. "I have to go. Perhaps we can dance together later Bryce."

"It was good to see you, Monique."

Savage satisfaction roared through Ciara. Bryce had come here with her, and despite Monique's advances, he'd sidestepped her invitation to dance. Of course, it helped show solidarity for their case if they remained together, her cynical side argued. Besides, Bryce had 'been there, done that' with his ex-girlfriend.

Still, Ciara wanted to shout her delight. Someone had picked *her* first!

The dinner tasted delicious but Ciara couldn't have said what they talked about. The small amount of wine she drank went to her head and made her feel dizzy. It couldn't be the man at her side whose rapt attention made her feel beautiful and desirable.

Despite her habitual doubts of why Bryce had brought her instead of the blondes he preferred, the glittering room, the beautiful view and Bryce's nearness caused a bubbling excitement inside her.

After the dishes were cleared away and the legal association business handled, the band began to play a slow melody. Bryce rose.

"Would you like to dance?"

Ciara smiled and stood at once. "I thought you'd never ask."

Bryce shared a nod with Durayev and led her to the floor to join the other couples there. He took her in his arms at last and pressed her against him. Her body felt breathless and overheated and shivery. She sighed with pleasure.

They glided around the floor. She'd been right about the similarity in heights. It aligned their bodies perfectly so his cock nestled against the notch of her thighs. His hand felt warm against her back. His other hand held hers in a strong, secure grip.

Ciara watched him watching her, his blue eyes laser sharp. Bryce was a man who knew what he wanted and went after it. He was mature. He'd been with confident women who knew what they wanted.

She was a confident woman. What did she want? For starters, she wanted Bryce to have no connection to Steele. But even being Steele's lawyer carried obligations, didn't it?

The slow ballad segued into a popular love song. Ciara couldn't look away from Bryce. His head dipped towards hers and she held her breath. But his attention snapped to someone dancing by. She glimpsed a tall blonde. He nodded at someone she couldn't see and the tension between them dissipated.

They danced every slow dance together until the band called it a night at eleven o'clock. By then she wanted to do a horizontal mamba with Bryce. He kept his warm hand at her back as they followed Durayev to the car.

"Thanks for inviting me, Bryce," Ciara said, her voice breathy.

"I'm glad you came." His was deep and husky.

"Me too."

As they reached their car, a man in the next car climbed out. The dome light illuminated his blonde wife.

"We can wait for AAA in the club house, Addison."

"You don't need another drink, John. We can wait right here."

"*I'm* going back inside. Are you coming?"

"No."

The man slammed the car door and stormed past them towards the clubhouse.

Durayev studied the woman, and then turned to Bryce. "I need to search the car."

"Do you really think the bomber would try here? We weren't followed."

"I'm not paid to take chances." Durayev dropped to the blacktop. A beam of light splayed from his hand over the undercarriage, back and forth. The light extinguished and Durayev climbed back to his feet. "All clear."

Bryce seated Ciara in the car and rounded the trunk. When the blonde in the next car gave him a once-over, Ciara wanted to claw her eyes out. As he climbed behind the wheel, the other woman smiled at him. What was she trying to do, make up for being angry with her own husband? Ciara glared at her.

A horrific boom rocked Ciara's head back against the headrest. Bryce's door slammed shut. Glass shattered. There was a whoosh, tremendous heat, and the roaring sound of flames.

CHAPTER 15

"Get out!" Bryce yelled at Ciara. My God, it was a bomb! His heart pounded like a trip hammer.

While Ciara fumbled with the door handle, Bryce unlatched her seat belt and pushed her. As the door swung open she nearly fell out of the car. He vaulted over the shift column into her empty seat. Flames licked at him through the glassless window. He tumbled out after her.

"Move! Our car could explode!" he ordered, and pulled her to her feet.

Ciara ran, but she turned to look over her shoulder and skidded to a stop, nearly falling.

"That woman!" she shrieked.

Bryce nearly barreled into her and grabbed her arm to steady her. "Get clear!"

He pivoted, dragging in breath. Men shouted from every side, women screamed, and car alarms wailed. Durayev had been by Bryce's door. He'd slammed it shut when the bomb blew. His body had hit the door a moment later. Bryce had to see if he lived.

But he'd only taken a step back towards the car when his rental blew up. The force knocked him down. Hot fiery metal rained down and he rolled over to protect his head and face. Thick acrid smoke billowed around him and he coughed. His lungs burned in his chest but he knew it wasn't from the fire. He fumbled in his pocket for his inhaler and raised it to his mouth with a shaking hand to take a quick drag.

A woman off to his left was sobbing.

"Bryce!" Ciara screamed. "Bryce! Are you all right?"

"Yeah," he managed. He was glad for the heat the hard asphalt beneath him retained from the long summer day.

The smoke cleared enough for him to see there was no way the woman in the other car could have survived. Swallowing bile, he looked away from a human shape in the flames. He didn't think Durayev lived either. There was something burning on the ground between the two car infernos.

Oh God. That could have been him and Ciara! His chest tightened with emotions he didn't have time to analyze.

A cool hand touched his cheek. "Bryce, can you talk?"

"Call nine-one-one." He dug in his suit jacket and handed her his phone.

As her shaking hands worked the phone, pounding feet raced to them. "Help's on the way! Are you hurt?" A young man in a waiter's black and white uniform dropped to his knees beside them.

"I've got scrapes and bruises," Ciara answered. "Bryce?"

"Asthma attack." He wheezed and took another hit from the inhaler using both hands. The waiter helped him sit up.

Assessing their injuries as non-life-threatening, the waiter turned to look at the blazing vehicles. "My God, what happened?"

"Bomb." Ciara handed him the phone with wildly shaking hands. "You'd better tell nine-one-one to send the police. Homicide. There was a woman in that car." Her voice hitched. "And our bodyguard is probably dead." She leaned against Bryce and he felt her trembling.

People gathered around them to stare at the fire with shocked faces. The spectators peppered one another with questions.

More shoes pounded on the pavement. "Addison!" a man's mortal cry rent the night.

Bystanders grabbed the husband and restrained him from throwing himself at the still-raging fires.

"Addison!" he screamed again.

Bryce flinched at the man's horrified expression. Guilt burned in Bryce's gut. His fault.

The waiter beside them relayed what he'd been told into the phone with only the slightest quaver in his voice.

"Tell the FBI too," Bryce said in his raspy voice. "Have them send Agent Pollack."

"The FBI?" The young man's voice rose in surprise at the end.

"They know the history of this case," Ciara explained, rubbing her arms. "Tell them someone's tried to murder Bryce Gannon again."

"Ciara." Bryce tried to caution her. He didn't want the world to know.

But the waiter was relaying what she'd said into the phone.

"Have them send the bomb squad," Ciara added belatedly.

"Bomb?" the husband repeated, his voice tortured. "This was a bomb?"

"Yes," Ciara gently told him.

"Someone set a bomb for you and killed my wife?" the man's voice rose in volume as he spoke.

"I'm sorry," Ciara said.

"Are you sorry?" the man demanded of Bryce.

"I'm very sorry for your loss," Bryce responded, his voice gravelly. His chest muscles tightened painfully.

"My loss." The man spat the word. "My wife, you mean. You'll bet you're sorry for her loss."

The bereaved husband advanced towards Bryce. Orange flames gave his angry eyes a demonic look. Two waiters grabbed his arms.

"Sir, you're not thinking clearly," the waiter on the left told him.

"I know a guilty party when I see one," the man raged, struggling against the restraining arms.

Sirens sliced the air. Bryce hope they hurried before the enraged husband finished what the bomber had started.

But the young waiters were stronger than they looked and finally the husband sank to the blacktop and began to cry in huge noisy sobs.

Bryce looked away, swallowing to ease the tightness in his throat. He could finally breathe easily, literally and figuratively. Now he could concentrate on more than moving air in and out of his lungs. His back and head hurt where he'd been thrown against the hard ground. His left elbow hurt. He thought he felt moisture there. Otherwise, he was alive and whole.

Ciara sat beside him. Her hair had loosened from its knot and the kinky dark curls hung past her shoulders. She looked younger that way. She also looked frightened. He gripped her bloodied hand and she gave him a strained smile.

"I think we'd better move back so the fire equipment can get in here," the waiter said. "Can the two of you stand yet?"

"If you pull me up," Ciara said.

Helping hands reached in to tug Ciara and Bryce to their feet, and then the remarkably calm young waiter urged everyone out of the way as a fire engine rumbled up. It gave a near-deafening horn blast to speed stragglers.

When the truck blocked Bryce's view of the burning pyre he gave a shaky sigh of relief.

The EMTs drove up behind the engine. Bryce snaked an arm around Ciara's waist. She was still trembling, so he drew her close.

"Anybody hurt?" an EMT yelled.

Helpful bystanders directed them to Bryce and Ciara. The EMTs cleaned and bandaged Ciara's bloodied knees and palms. They had to help Bryce out of his suit jacket. Blood stained his white shirt scarlet around a rip in his left elbow. They cut his shirt off at the bicep and went to work.

"I don't think you need stitches," the EMT informed Bryce.

"Thank God." The last thing Bryce needed was another trip to the ER.

"You might want to go to the hospital to have your head and back x-rayed, just to be safe," the EMT added.

Ciara opened her mouth, but Bryce glared her to silence. "I'll see my doctor."

"Okay, but you might have a painful weekend."

"I'll take my chances."

"Seems like I heard you say that before."

Bryce turned at Pollack's voice to see him and Garrison. Bryce felt almost relieved. He let out his breath. "You guys beat the metro cops here."

"All the better for you, right?"

"I won't say I'm not glad to see you."

"Where's your security?" Garrison asked, looking around.

"Dead. I hope the bomb killed him because I'd hate to think he burned to death like the innocent bystander did."

"Damn," Pollack swore. "The bomber's got a serious hard-on for you."

"Yeah. He's either getting smarter or he knew I had a bodyguard who searched my car for bombs. He blew up the car next to us with enough explosives that we got caught in the chain reaction." Bryce coughed.

The EMT eyed him. "You didn't mention smoke inhalation. You really should let the hospital check you out."

"No," Bryce said firmly, waving him away. "The couple in the car next to us said something about car trouble."

"So the bomber knows how to disable cars," Pollack said. "And he had to watch to see when you got into your car."

"Remote control," Garrison agreed. "May still be around."

"Long gone I'm sure," his partner said.

Garrison glanced around, and then asked, "Are you and Miss Alafita okay?"

Bryce nodded.

"Nothing serious," Ciara added. "But we could have died!" She shuddered.

The EMT laid a blanket around her shoulders. She pulled it tight. "This has got to stop! He's going to get lucky and kill Bryce! And me."

"The offer of the safe house still stands," Pollack said.

"As much as running away appeals to me, how safe is it really?" Bryce asked. "How long until the bomber or his associates know I'm there? I'd be a sitting duck."

Ciara's face lit with excitement. "Bryce, I know a place you can hide!"

With Steele's own spy?

"Miss Alafita, we can't guarantee anyplace else," Garrison said.

"But it's perfect. No one would think to look for you there," Ciara went on undeterred.

"I'm not going to Adam Steele's house," Bryce remarked a little acidly. He clenched his jaw against saying too much.

"Not his house. Mine," she said in smug triumph.

"Your hotel is hardly private," he scoffed.

"In Lansing."

Bryce felt flummoxed. Pollack and Garrison looked at one another.

"No one would look for you there, that's for sure," Pollack said.

Lansing. Where Ciara kept her secrets. A house far from the bomber. A weekend of peace and quiet . . . alone with Ciara. As his thoughts tumbled one after the other, his heartbeat sped up.

"Yeah," Bryce agreed. He looked up as the local police pulled in. "But only the four of us will know. No one else. No one at your office or mine. And not Adam Steele. Ciara and I drop off the face of the earth for the weekend. After we answer police questions, you can drive us home. I need some things from my house and Ciara needs her car."

"Bryce, wouldn't it be better if we left right from my hotel?" she asked.

"I can't wear this all weekend, can I?" He waved at his suit. "Besides, if anyone is watching the Feds, they'll expect me to go home."

"That still leaves you unprotected from the time you arrive home from Lansing until you reach the courthouse Monday morning," Garrison reminded Bryce.

"I'm sure one of Steele's people will have my house staked out when I return home."

"How do you know it won't be someone sent to kill you?" Pollack asked.

"I'll call Steele when I'm thirty minutes from my house."

"Steele's a smart man. What makes you think he won't figure out Miss Alafita's address in Lansing?" Garrison asked.

Bryce looked at Ciara. "I believe he'll think I'm safe there."

They finished outlining their plan, and then Bryce and Ciara gave their statements to the police. Pollack and Garrison drove them home, and within an hour Bryce and Ciara were speeding west through the inky blackness towards Lansing.

CHAPTER 16

Ciara let Bryce into her Lansing condo and watched him look around the pristine, modern kitchen. Nerves fluttered in her stomach. They'd made the ninety-minute drive mostly in silence with the windows rolled down to scour away the smell of smoke. Now they had to speak to each other.

"I have a spare bedroom. No one ever uses it," she offered.

Bryce turned and placed his hand on her arm. "I don't want to sleep alone. I nearly died tonight. So did you."

Ciara swallowed. Her heart raced like an Indy car. "I don't want to sleep alone either."

His serious blue eyes bored into hers. "We can just sleep if you want to. We're both exhausted. We don't have to make love."

Oh God. As soon as he said the words her body came alive, her loins clenching with need. "I want to make love with you."

Bryce smiled, the expression small and almost sad. "We need to shower."

"And get our bandages wet?"

"Oh, right." He looked at her bandaged hands. "This is going to be awkward."

"Necessity is the mother of invention," Ciara said. She locked the door to the garage, took Bryce's hand and led him through her ranch-style condo to the master bedroom.

"Ladies first." Bryce waved at the attached bathroom.

Ciara took her overnight bag into the bathroom. Damn, but she wished she'd known she was going to make love tonight. She wouldn't have fallen on her hands, for one thing. She stripped off her smoky clothes, brushed her teeth, and tried to think of a way to wash without getting her hands wet.

Bryce knocked on the door. "Ciara? If you changed your mind, it's okay."

What?! Ciara snatched the door open and her mouth dried. Bryce wore only navy briefs that faithfully outlined his masculine attributes. And he had attributes!

"God, you're perfect!" His voice was hoarse.

She remembered her own nakedness then, and remembered he preferred buxom blondes. But the erection straining his briefs told her he liked what he saw. Her nipples peaked in response.

Bryce reached out to caress one aching tip with his fingertips. The nipple furled tighter. "No, you didn't change your mind."

"I want to wash my face, and you know, but . . . " She held up her hands.

He stepped into the bathroom, crowding her against the sink. Her flesh tingled everywhere it touched his warm, hard body. He reached past her to turn on the warm water, then he grabbed the washcloth she'd laid beside the sink and let the water soak it. He wrung it out and reached up to her face.

He paused. "May I?"

"Sure," she choked out.

Gently he scrubbed her face with the warm washcloth, removing her make-up. What he saw now was the real thing. He studied her, and then rinsed the cloth. He washed her face again and her neck. She'd never had a man care for her or do anything personal like this for her. She felt . . . cherished.

Ciara looked up into Bryce's heated blue eyes. His face was tight with desire. He rinsed the washcloth again and scrubbed it over his own face and neck. She watched with wonder as his strong, sure hands performed this ordinary task. His hands, face, and neck were masculine, his body tight with lean muscles that flexed smoothly as he moved.

He laid the cloth on the counter and stripped out of his briefs. His engorged cock sprang free. It was just as large and thick as she'd imagined. Her lower body clenched. She wanted it inside her.

Then Bryce washed them both intimately. Ciara didn't know what turned her on more, his touch on her body or his taking care of her. When he reached for her she went eagerly into his arms. His mouth came down on hers. He tasted slightly mediciney. His firm lips ate at hers and she ravished his in return. She'd never had a man kiss her like he did, like he couldn't stop.

Ciara pressed her breasts against his firm chest and her hips against his erection. He raised her onto her tiptoes and slid his cock between her legs.

She moaned into his mouth. He slid his cock back and forth along her increasingly wet folds, echoing the thrust of his tongue into her mouth. Their tongues dueled. His hands molded the curves of her bottom. She imagined him lifting her into his deep thrusts and her pussy clenched hard.

She broke the kiss to urge, "Fill me."

"I want to do things to your body to make you beg."

"Fill me," she said. "We have all weekend to do the rest."

Bryce looked intently at her and she stared back. She knew what he sought—that she wasn't doing this just because they'd escaped death. That her mind was clear.

He nodded. "Next time then."

Bryce pulled her into the bedroom, grabbed a condom from his overnight bag, and led them to her bed. Ciara helped him sheathe his cock in the latex. She pulled back the covers and then he pushed her onto the bed and followed her down.

When Bryce mounted her, Ciara's nerves fluttered. This was Bryce Gannon, cold lawyer and possible mobster's tool who preferred blondes and didn't make lifetime commitments.

Her eyes must have betrayed her thoughts, for he halted.

Ciara looked into Bryce's warm blue eyes and saw the man she'd worked beside for a week, a man who struggled against any sign of weakness, a man who valued control, a man with deep passion he kept locked inside. And she was in a perfect position to unlock it. She smiled.

"Was that second thoughts?" he asked quietly.

"There's no going back once we do this."

"No, there isn't."

She wrapped her legs around his hips. "Then what are you waiting for?"

"Yes, Counselor."

Bryce pushed slowly but inexorably inside her. It had been awhile, so her body protested.

"You're so tight. I don't want to hurt you."

Bryce pressed forward into her until finally she was filled. It felt so good she surged against him, driving him even deeper. She gasped.

"Again," she begged.

He withdrew and surged into her again, which drew another gasp. Within a few strokes she had his rhythm and they thrust against one another over and over. The sound of their gasps and groans resounded in her bedroom as she and Bryce strained to give and receive pleasure.

Their bodies grew slick with sweat. Then she realized what Bryce was doing. He hadn't lost control.

"Bryce, I've wanted to do this with you for a week."

He jerked and stared at her. Only a thin circle of blue remained surrounding his darkened pupils.

"I couldn't stop thinking about making love with you, how good it would feel."

"I wanted you too," he admitted. "And then you played basketball in that skirt. God, my pants were too tight." He plunged harder.

"I want to muss your hair, to run my hands all over your body, and then use my mouth on you."

"God!" He thrust so deep she screamed.

And then she was coming apart inside, spasming her release. He shouted with his, jerking rhythmically deep inside her.

Bryce collapsed onto her with a groan. Ciara enfolded him in her arms. She vowed he would never be able to come to her bed again and hold onto his control.

"About that mussing," he murmured.

"Next time, I swear under oath."

"We have a lot of next times."

"We don't have to get out of bed if we don't want to."

She was feeling decidedly relaxed and sinking into the mattress. They were safe and she had Bryce right where she wanted him.

"I don't want to." Bryce sounded sleepy.

"Me neither. How long do you need to recover?"

"Ask me later."

"Hmm." Thoughts were becoming harder. Bryce was a warm weight on her, his breath gusting past her bare shoulder. Her legs slid off his hips to land on the mattress. Later.

• • •

There were many laters and many next times. Bryce couldn't stop discovering parts of Ciara he wanted to kiss, touch, lick, rub, or make love to. And how they made love! Except for Ciara running to the store for condoms and food, they barely left her bed Saturday.

He wasn't a young man, but he only had to look at her to want her. She acted the same. This was stolen time, time when each of them ignored their obligations to other people and concentrated on each other.

Ciara was beautiful. He'd known it from the moment he saw her. But she was even more beautiful naked. And sexy. He realized that making love to her was more than sex. She'd gotten closer than any woman he'd dated. She'd made him think and feel things he hadn't previously. He thought about having a wife he loved who loved him in return, one who was his equal in every way. He thought about having children he could play with, about having a legal partner. And he thought about being mussed—not just in sexual passion but also in passion for life. He'd been caged since the hazing in college. Maybe it was time he broke out and lived a little.

Saturday evening they ate grilled steaks and salad for dinner while the rain from the latest thunderstorm trailed off to a drizzle. Bryce had barely noticed the predicted storms roll through during the day. He felt pleasantly tired physically, but his mind needed exercise. And he needed some time with his oxygen tank.

"Do you mind if I work for a little while?" he asked.

Ciara started the dishwasher and looked up. "Are you tired of me already?"

Although her tone was light, he sensed something more serious underlying the question. He wrapped her in his arms and kissed her.

"Not tired of you. Just feeling my age. I need to recharge my batteries. For later."

Ciara smiled, satisfaction and seduction mixed together. "Then by all means recharge."

Bryce gave her another swift kiss and then retrieved the box of files from her car. He settled on her comfortable fabric couch with the box on the coffee table in front of him and his oxygen cannula on. He'd used the oxygen while she'd gone to the store, but hadn't said anything to her about it. He braced himself for when she'd notice.

She hadn't packed anything in her house and he hadn't seen any boxes anywhere. Maybe she intended to let the movers handle everything, but it nagged at him. Everything was intact in the kitchen too. In fact, as he glanced around, it didn't appear that anything was missing. What had she taken to the hotel?

A flash of red caught his attention as Ciara moved around the kitchen setting things to rights. Those red gym shorts made her legs look a mile long. He'd had them wrapped around him while they made love so he knew how long they really were. And that white tank top revealed rather than hid her breasts. She wore no bra and her dark nipples showed as shadows while the ribbed tank lovingly cupped the round globes. That shirt should be X-rated.

He smiled. If he stared at her much longer they were going back to bed sooner than he'd thought possible. He looked down at the couch. They hadn't made love here yet. Or on the kitchen table.

"Bryce, I thought you were going to work."

"You're distracting me."

Ciara walked into the living room and stepped between him and the coffee table. She placed one hand on the couch beside him and with the other reached down to feel his cock through his shorts.

"You're not really distracted."

"I'm working on it."

He held his breath waiting for her reaction to the oxygen, but she didn't say a word. His breath whooshed out and he hauled her down for a grateful kiss. She groped him without mercy. But he couldn't get a full hard-on yet.

"You really are tired," she said with concern in her voice and on her face.

"Only for a little while. Are you disappointed?"

"God, no, Bryce! I'm just as happy to be here with you and look at you. And touch you. I love your hair this way." She ran her hands through the gel-free strands. They'd managed a shower earlier. "It's such a warm color."

Bryce pulled her into his lap. Ciara straddled him and he wrapped his arms around her.

"You have such passion," he said.

"So do you."

He shook his head. "I feel half alive. I've felt that way most of my life." He took a deep breath of oxygen and looked into her warm brown eyes. "This isn't the first time someone's tried to kill me." Ciara gasped, and he continued. "I've run track since boarding school, so when I went to college I wanted to join the fraternity where the track team members belonged. I thought having a common interest would help me fit in with them.

"They seemed to accept me, although I learned later they were only pretending. They thought because I was . . . dispassionate . . . that I was a rich snob, and they decided to teach me a lesson that I didn't belong. They hazed me during fraternity initiation week. They trapped me in a wooden cage, threw it in a nearby lake, and left me there to die. One of them yelled, 'See if your money can buy you out of that, rich boy,' as they walked away laughing."

Ciara gripped his biceps hard, her face pale as she listened to his account.

"I would have drowned. The cage was too heavy for me to lift from inside it. It pushed me under as it sank. I knew the frat boys weren't coming back to help me."

"Obviously you escaped." Her voice was strained.

Bryce nodded. "Paul Ziko saved me. He'd figured out the frat boys weren't my friends. He led Roger Barrett and Sean Bergman to me, and the three of them pulled me out of the water. I barely knew Paul—we weren't even friends—but he saved my life."

"And you've remained friends since then."

"Yeah. You find out who you can trust when your life is in danger. But I also learned that cruel people prey on those who appear weak or vulnerable. I swore I'd never let anybody see me that way again. I'd be strong, and I'd be a winner. But by not showing my emotions on the outside, now I only feel alive on the inside when I'm winning."

"Bryce, you have plenty of passion inside you. I don't think anyone's challenged you outside of the courtroom. You've been surrounded by yes men."

"You're certainly not one of those."

"You *need* challenges. You thrive on them. I've been good for you that way."

"You certainly have." He wanted to ask her then about Steele. Wanted the truth out in the open so they could move forward. But the thought of shattering their idyll made him shudder. He didn't want this time to end.

Ciara kissed him gently. "Finish your work. I have plans for you later."

"I've got plans for you too."

"Me first."

"I always let you come first."

"Bryce."

She climbed off his lap and took those long legs out of sight. His lap missed her.

He pulled out files and his notes. He had to have missed something he could twist to his advantage. This box of facts was all he had to work with. There was no more time to investigate, and no opportunity, not while they were hiding. He'd won nearly every case he'd tried in the past few years. This was a case he *had* to win . . . for the prosecution.

CHAPTER 17

Guilt ate at Ciara as she glanced back once at Bryce before she headed to the spare bedroom where her Internet connection was located. He'd turned his full attention to the Steele files.

Bryce was so careful not to let other people see him use his oxygen or his inhaler, and now she knew why. He didn't trust other people easily. He feared showing weakness to anyone who might use it against him, as the college fraternity boys had. That he'd felt comfortable enough now in her presence to do so was a declaration of trust.

But his trust was misplaced. She bit her lip. She didn't want lies between them, not after what they'd shared together. Not after he'd confided the hazing to her. She hadn't found any record of that when she'd researched him, so he'd kept quiet about it. Until he'd told her. She was as bad as the frat boys with their deceit, waiting to trap him and take him down, to use his secrets and his weaknesses against him. She had to tell him the truth. But she wanted one more day with Bryce. This time with him was precious.

Resolved that she'd tell him the truth tomorrow before they returned to Detroit, Ciara turned on her laptop. She'd make the most of the time they had left.

• • •

Two hours of poring through the facts unearthed little that could help Bryce. Frustration ate at him. He didn't want Steele to own him. Hell, if Bryce could, he'd break Ciara free of Steele and the two of them could run a lot farther than Lansing.

Bryce pushed the box away. Dammit. He must be more tired than he thought because he couldn't think of a way he could lose. The house was dim outside his pool of light, and quiet. Had Ciara fallen asleep waiting for him? Well he'd just have to wake her. He was up for making love again. He set the oxygen aside feeling energized once more.

He found her in the spare bedroom at her computer. She looked up guiltily at his step and blanked the screen. Every instinct he had roared to life propelling him forward into the room. Anger heated his skin and sped his pulse. He reached over her shoulder and jabbed the screen back on. He expected to see an e-mail from Steele or something else incriminating.

Instead he found . . . "Personal lubricants?" He felt shell-shocked.

Ciara's color was high. "I'm a little dry. I wanted to see what we could use. I didn't want you to know, to think less of me."

He caged her in her chair. "Ciara, I don't think less of you. How could I when it's my fault? If you can't make love—"

"No! Bryce, I want to. There's something we can do to make it easier, even with a lubricant. It says so in this article."

"Anything."

She licked her lips. Her pulse point in her throat was jumping madly. "Bryce, we can make love without a condom. I'm clean, and I'm on the pill, I swear it."

Not use a condom? He'd never done that. Bryce stepped away from her and sank onto the spare bed, staring into her dark eyes. He rubbed his palms on his shorts. He'd never taken chances, not with his health, and not with bringing a child into the world like that. Ciara was asking him to take a chance on her, to trust her. Hadn't he just thought the worst when she blanked her computer screen? He didn't trust her about Steele.

But he trusted her with his body. He'd come to Lansing, to her home, and made love to her. He'd fallen asleep in her arms. She didn't lie to him with her body. And he'd told her his biggest secret. That took even more trust.

Thinking about making love to her stirred his cock to life once more. He wanted to feel the moist warmth of Ciara's body on his sensitive flesh, wanted it so much he was aching hard that fast.

Ciara had waited. She seemed to know when he needed to think about things. Now she asked, "Are you clean?"

"Yes, definitely."

"It says baby oil works, preferably unscented."

God, the visions that initiated! He licked his dry lips. "Do you have plastic wrap?"

Ciara laughed. "You want to do something kinky?"

"Hell, yes. Where's the baby oil?"

"In the bathroom."

"I'll get it. Bring the plastic wrap. Meet me back here."

"Not in my bed?"

"If we're using baby oil, let's use the spare bed."

"Right."

• • •

They met back in the spare bedroom. Bryce was naked, his taut body beautiful in the lamp's glow. His erection thrust proudly against his abdomen. Ciara's lower body clenched in anticipation. No matter how many times she saw him naked, she wanted him.

Ciara helped him spread the plastic wrap across the bed. It didn't want to stay put until they overlapped several sheets. When there was a good-sized rectangle, Bryce squirted baby oil over it.

Gingerly, Ciara climbed onto the plastic, sliding a little on the oil. The plastic crackled as she moved. Bryce climbed onto the bed, and he slid too. An unfamiliar, girlish giggle escaped her lips. They rediscovered one another's bodies with slippery fingers. And Ciara discovered something else. Bryce could have fun while making love. She didn't have time to examine the wonder of this unexpected side of him before the need to have him inside of her became critical.

As Bryce fitted himself to her, he paused, "Are you sure?"

She knew what he was asking. She wanted this. "Yes."

Slowly he slid inside. She felt his warm bare flesh fill her aching need in a delicious glide. The deeper he pushed, the worse the ache became.

He groaned. "Ah, God, it feels good."

Ciara groaned too. She'd never felt anything so good or so intimate.

They made love with an intensity that belied all the times that had gone before. When they lay panting and trembling afterward, she felt absolutely shaken. She didn't ever want to make love with any man but Bryce ever again. God, what had she done?

Bryce didn't want her for a lifetime commitment. He didn't feel the significance of what they'd done. She hadn't realized what she'd wanted when she'd asked him to have unprotected sex. Now she did and it rocked her.

Ciara clasped Bryce to her trying not to let him know how desperate she felt.

"Hang on, Ciara. Gimme a minute to recover. Then we're doing that again."

Hope rose in her heart. She had the rest of the weekend with him. There was still time.

• • •

Bryce watched Ciara pace the basketball court sidelines yelling instructions and encouragement to the teenaged girls on the church team she coached. She glowed with vitality and happiness.

He'd like to think he'd put that look on her face, him and his lovemaking. But this was Ciara in her element. She *thrived*—it was the only word to describe it. And because of this weekend with her, he was thriving too. He'd never felt so relaxed and yet so alive. And happy.

Ciara called the girls to her and they huddled together while the other church team did the same with their coach. Young faces turned to Ciara like flowers to the sun. Was that the effect she had on him too?

The girls were losing, but not by a large margin. He watched them play with their hearts in it, as Ciara did. The other team was better and Ciara's girls were outclassed, but that didn't stop them.

Bryce was one of a handful of spectators, so it was even a greater achievement that the girls played all out with no one to cheer them on.

It was no surprise when they lost, although they bounced on their heels around Ciara like eager puppies. The young black woman, Sonya Harding, who also coached, beamed at the girls. She was hugely pregnant and unable to do more than waddle slowly on the court. The cacophony of high-pitched voices carried them out of the church's gymnasium into the hot summer day.

The girls drifted away one by one, some walked home, and some were picked up in cars, and a few went home with one of the spectators. Then it was just Sonya and the two of them.

"Ciara, I'm so glad you came." Sonya clasped Ciara's hands. "And not just so I could sit down during the game."

"Not much longer," Ciara said.

"No, thank the Lord. And thank goodness we've only got one game left. This heat is murder."

"I can't promise I'll make the next one, but I'll try."

"Bless you. You two have a safe drive back." Sonya gave them a knowing look. "It was nice to meet you, Bryce."

"Same here, Sonya."

As they drove back to Ciara's condo, Bryce mentioned as casually as he could, "I never thought about coaching young people before. I've been a runner for years, so I could probably coach track." He waited to hear what Ciara said.

She glanced at him. "I find it very rewarding, especially working with underprivileged kids. You probably would too. All some of them need is encouragement."

"Yeah, that's what I thought when I was watching your team play. There must be young runners who need guidance. I'm a winner. I'm sure I could teach others to win."

"I'm sure you could." Ciara studied the road for a long moment. "I could help you improve your basketball skills. One on one is a good way to stay in shape. Almost as good as running."

Bryce observed her while she watched the road. It was between them, the unspoken knowledge that he probably would never run again. But his heart didn't speed up in fear and panic as it had in the hospital, because she was offering him energetic alternatives that would help him return to being healthy and strong.

She'd shown him this weekend that he'd lost nothing of his male potency. Now she'd shown him she didn't think of him as a victim. A smile tugged at the corner of his lips.

"Thank you. I'd like that."

When they returned to her condo they made love slowly and with poignancy. This was their last night together. Who knew what tomorrow might bring? Bryce didn't want this time with Ciara to end—the sharing and the knowing he wasn't alone. He needed this.

Even if it wasn't real.

"Let's go out to dinner," Ciara suggested afterwards.

"I like having you to myself." He didn't want the outside world to intrude again.

"I know this little Italian restaurant twenty minutes from here that has chicken Marsala that melts in your mouth. And the chocolate torte for dessert—"

"I see the truth now. The chicken probably tastes like rubber. You want the chocolate."

"Of course."

He squeezed her tight. "We have so little time left together."

"We have all night, Bryce."

"Part of the night. We should start back around four A.M."

"We have enough time. And I can stay at your house."

Bryce held her at arm's length. "No. Steele's bodyguard will be there. I don't want him to know."

She frowned. "What does it matter?"

"It matters."

Ciara held him tight and one thing led to another. They headed for dinner several hours later wearing casual clothes.

The chicken Marsala was just as delicious as Ciara had said it was. Bryce plied her with a glass of wine to get her to relax. She seemed overly bright and a little brittle. Maybe he shouldn't have refused to let her stay the night at his house. But he'd wanted more time before Steele found out they were lovers.

They shared the chocolate torte and got a little messy feeding each other. Bryce thought of wicked things they could do with this dessert and two naked, hungry bodies. He filed the thought away for the future. Then he was startled that he thought he'd ever come back to Lansing, and with Ciara. Was he hoping for something long-term with her? Since everything depended on the Steele trial, he shook off the thought.

Bryce excused himself to wash up and when he returned he found a tall, dark-haired man speaking to Ciara.

"Are you through with the assignment then? Is Gannon corrupt or not?"

"Mr. Baisden, I—"

Bryce moved into Ciara's line of sight and she flushed guiltily and stopped speaking.

Baisden, the Attorney General. She was reporting to the AG on *him*. Betrayal punched Bryce in the gut.

CHAPTER 18

Ciara had betrayed Bryce's trust. She was a liar and a deceiver. And here was irrefutable evidence. Bryce felt hot and then cold, and pain radiated from the region of his heart.

The attorney general turned, following Ciara's gaze to Bryce. "Gannon. You're looking better than the last time I saw you." He didn't look the least bit guilty.

Bryce glanced from Baisden to Ciara and an awful realization hit him. Anger made his skin flush with heat.

"When was that?"

"When you were in the ICU."

When he was at his most vulnerable. His fists clenched. "And that's when you sent your spy to me." Ciara gasped and Bryce glared at her. "I knew you were a spy, but I thought you were Steele's."

"Steele's! Why would you think that?"

"You showed up within hours of him telling me I couldn't refuse his case, that he had eyes everywhere. And then there you were. Just someone else to betray me. Those UM frat boys could take lessons from you." His bitter, angry tone amazed him. Where was his cold detachment?

"Bryce, I was going to tell you the truth."

Bryce ignored that, addressing the AG instead. "And Baisden, I thought you were corrupt because she was."

"Hardly," Baisden scoffed.

"Well, Ciara, if you don't know the answer to the AG's question, you don't know me at all."

"But you're defending Adam Steele."

"He made me an offer I couldn't refuse." Bryce had never felt so cold inside, not even when he realized the truth about the frat boys.

He strode to the other side of the table and held out his hand to Ciara. "If you have a spare key, I'll clear out my stuff and get out of your life."

"Bryce, you can't go back to Detroit now. They'll kill you."

"They can try. Do you have a spare key or not?"

Ciara stood. "I'll drive you."

"Don't bother. I'm sure you and your real boss have things to discuss. I see why you wanted to come here tonight."

Ciara's face reddened. "That wasn't the reason."

"Make sure you tell him you slept with me as ordered."

Ciara jerked and said stonily, "That was spiteful. You owe me an apology."

Bryce felt a spurt of guilt. They'd shared a beautiful weekend together. Then he remembered *he* was the one who'd been betrayed. "I believe it's the other way around. Who spied on whom? Who lied to whom?" The words echoed eerily.

"I ordered her to," Baisden interjected. "I have to protect the public."

Bryce gave the AG his coldest stare. "The end justifies the means?"

"In this case, yes."

"It's difficult to tell the alleged good guys from the bad when you both use the same dirty tactics."

Ciara gasped. Baisden frowned at Bryce. Bryce continued to hold out his hand.

She handed Bryce her keys. "Take my car. I'll get a cab home."

Bryce wanted to refuse, but the quicker he got away from Ciara the better. He felt his chest tightening with a stress-triggered asthma attack. "I'll leave the keys inside the back door."

"You can drive it to Detroit."

"I wouldn't want the bomber to blow up your car. I'll find another way home."

Bryce pivoted and left them behind, his lover and her puppet master. He climbed behind the wheel of her Camry, used his inhaler and then carefully headed back to her house. Thank God he'd paid attention on the drive here. The unfamiliarity of the city required all his concentration, so ruthlessly he shoved away what had happened in the restaurant.

After parking in her garage, Bryce called Enterprise Rent-A-Car, who promised to deliver a car within thirty minutes. He gathered all the Steele files and carried the box to the front door. Then he went in the bedroom and packed. The room smelled strongly of sex, the bed was wrecked, the pillows dented by two heads close together. The pain in his chest felt like a gaping wound.

Bryce forced himself to look away, to go in the bathroom and gather his things. His toiletries had become mixed with hers, his razor and comb in her medicine cabinet. He struggled with his breathing, fighting off another attack.

His gaze fell on the box of condoms in the medicine cabinet. His fists clenched. He hoped Ciara hadn't lied about being on the pill because they hadn't used any other protection since yesterday. He hadn't wanted anything between his skin and hers after the first time they made love that way.

He'd been an all-around fool.

By the time the rented Ford Fusion drove into the driveway, Bryce had double checked Ciara's house to make sure he hadn't left anything behind. His chest tightened painfully as he looked around the condo, his hand on the doorknob. The truth that she lived *here*, not in Detroit, had stared him right in the face, but he'd ignored his instincts and let lust blind him.

He'd proven once again his feelings couldn't be trusted. Bryce opened the door and crossed the threshold. After he loaded the car, he left Ciara's keys between the two doors. He dropped the Enterprise driver off and began the trek to Detroit. As he accelerated onto the freeway and engaged the cruise control, he gave his feelings free reign: anger, betrayal, hurt, fear, loss. His stomach knotted, his throat tightened and the road blurred before his eyes. This was worse than the hazing. Yes, those young men had pretended to be his friends, but they hadn't slept with him.

They hadn't made him fall in love with them.

Bryce knew it was true. Despite all his reservations about Ciara—well founded after all—he'd grown to like and trust her enough to sleep with her. And he'd fallen in love with her. She'd led him there. She'd studied him while he lay unconscious in the ICU. She'd had days to learn about him before she came to him in the hospital. And she'd done her homework well. He hadn't even known he had wants and needs like those she'd unearthed. She'd played him as only one who knew someone well could.

Damn, damn, and damn. He nearly crushed the steering wheel in his bruising grip.

He'd finally found that elusive emotion after all these years, only to have it snatched away from him because the woman didn't love him in return.

Bryce was going home to his empty house, his empty life, his empty bed, and tomorrow he had to go into court alone. She'd ruined his perfectly ordered life, damn her.

• • •

"So that was the ruthless Bryce Gannon. He didn't seem so cold and dispassionate," Baisden remarked after Bryce left. "He sounded like a lover scorned."

As he turned back to her, Ciara tried to control her face, but his raised eyebrows and knowing look said she'd failed.

"You slept with him."

Ciara nodded, her cheeks burning.

He studied her. "Not as part of your investigation though."

"No, I wouldn't do that." She swallowed. "I think I'm in love with him."

"From that scene, I'd say he thought he was in love with you too."

"'Was' being the operative word," Ciara said, her tone unwontedly bitter. Her stomach twisted, upsetting her dinner. She should have confessed to Bryce yesterday. Now it was too late.

"Why don't we sit down? You can debrief while I'm here."

Baisden took Bryce's seat and Ciara sat back down. Baisden called his wife to say he'd need longer to pick up dinner and he'd explain when he got home.

"Now," he settled back in his chair. "Tell me about Bryce Gannon. You knew him well enough to become intimate with him."

What did Ciara know about Bryce? He was hardworking nearly to the point of being a workaholic because he wanted to win so badly. He had expensive tastes but he didn't live an ostentatious life. He had a core group of friends, but kept employees and everyone else at arm's length. He seemed lonely, but she couldn't explain exactly why she felt that way except what he'd said yesterday about being half alive.

Bryce hated weakness and vulnerability. He hated to be pitied. He'd kept himself healthy and active. He was meticulous. He didn't like showing emotion. He'd perfected the cold brush-off and the 'I don't care' exterior. He had a deep core of passion he kept under ruthless control but couldn't seem to control around her.

He made love to her like a man desperate to mate, to make her want him with the same unceasing need. He was a generous lover but he also consumed. She didn't tell that part to her boss, but she was sure her furiously blushing face told its own story.

Ciara told Baisden everything that had happened in the past few days. She told him about Bryce's judicial aspirations and the bombing Friday night.

And then she remembered, "He thought I was Steele's spy!" Her breath caught.

"That's some intuition he has to know you were a spy."

And still he'd slept with her, as though he couldn't help it. As though some part of him sensed he could trust some part of her.

"That's the answer!" Ciara exclaimed. Her heart pounded with excitement. "He's not corrupt. A corrupt man wouldn't think the man he was defending would have to spy on him."

"He said he'd tried to refuse the case," Baisden recalled. "But Steele called him in the hospital and made him an offer he couldn't refuse."

"Like something bad would happen to him there, and Bryce barely able to walk."

Baisden frowned. "A man who bows to threats isn't an asset on the bench."

"We don't know what the threat was."

"It doesn't make a difference what it was. Adam Steele knows he can bend Gannon to his will, so Gannon won't be any good as a judge."

Ciara knew the AG was wrong, but she didn't know why. "Bryce is fiercely independent. He's never worked with anyone his equal. He doesn't like being told what to do. Pretend you're him and you've just been forced to take a case you don't want to take. What would you do?"

Baisden's eyes narrowed. "He caved."

"I think he pretended to cave. Remember, he thought I worked for Steele, that I reported everything he did to Steele." Ciara's mind slowly turned over those words. Her mouth dropped open in surprise. "My God, he thought he was being watched every day. Then when Steele sent him security, he thought he was being observed twenty-four seven. He didn't trust me, the police, the Feds, or his security, and his friends have their own troubles. He couldn't ask anyone for help and he couldn't do much physically. What would you do in his position?"

"Are you suggesting he had a hidden agenda? That while dodging bombs, spies and traitors Gannon made and possibly executed a plan against Adam Steele? I'd say you were dreaming."

"My gut says that's what he's doing."

"Your gut couldn't tell me if Gannon was corrupt when I asked you a few minutes ago."

"I trusted him enough to sleep with him. I haven't trusted a man like that in a long time."

Baisden studied her for several long moments. "Bring me proof that he didn't cave to threats. I need more than a feeling."

"Bryce won't let me near the defense, not now. I'll have to watch the trial from the gallery. I'll have to drive back to Detroit tonight."

"I'll drive you home. Let me place my order so I don't arrive home late *and* empty handed."

• • •

Bryce drove southeast towards night. The setting sun proved a perfect corollary to his current situation. An hour out of Detroit he called Agent Pollack.

"It's Bryce Gannon. ETA Detroit sixty minutes."

"What happened?" Pollack demanded.

"Not what you think. Miss Alafita works for the Attorney General. He's investigating me for corruption."

"Ouch."

"Yeah. Listen, you know I have to call Steele."

"You think you have to."

"I need to know something. If these guys succeed in killing me, will you go after Steele's organization?"

Pollack hesitated. "Why do you ask?"

"I don't want to die, but if I do, I want it to do some good. Would you pursue Steele's organization to find the hitter and the person who ordered it?"

"Damn straight."

Bryce released his breath. "Good. I've made some notes. I'm going to swing by Paul Ziko's apartment and leave them with him just in case."

"Why not turn the information over to us now? We can help."

"This is the only way."

Pollack gave a loud sigh. "You'll probably see us around the courthouse tomorrow."

"I'll look forward to it."

Next Bryce called Paul Ziko.

"Bryce, where the hell have you been?" Paul yelled. "We've been worried sick. Are you in protective custody?"

"Hiding out, actually. Listen, I need to leave an envelope with you for safekeeping. Can I bring it by in about forty minutes?"

"Sure. You know you don't have to ask."

"Don't tell anyone you talked to me."

"Roger and Sean deserve to know. And Christian."

"Fine, but wait until I get there."

Bryce waited thirty minutes before he called Steele. When he was put through to the mobster, Steele's voice was glacial.

"I'm wondering where you disappeared to and whose company you've been keeping the past forty-eight hours."

Bryce realized he was relieved Ciara wasn't Steele's pipeline. His heartache lessened. "I watched your man die and that poor woman burn to death. I couldn't risk anyone else's life. I just needed to get away. I'm on my way home now. I'll be there in about an hour."

"You haven't used your credit card this weekend."

"Cash still spends in this world. I called to say I'm ready for trial."

There was a momentary pause. "I'd wondered that too. I'm glad you honor your commitments. I'll send security to your house."

"I'd rather not see anyone else killed."

"Mr. Durayev's job was to keep you alive. He did that. His death was unfortunate."

Bryce sighed. He'd known it wasn't any use to argue. "I'll see you in court tomorrow."

The die was cast. Bryce hoped Steele handpicked whomever he sent. There'd been enough attempts to kill Bryce that Steele had to wonder who was behind them.

Bryce drove to Paul's apartment in Royal Oak, not too far from his own house. Paul dragged him inside and hugged him hard. Bryce gripped his friend hard in return.

"Damn it, Bryce. Give up this case. It's not worth your life!" Paul said with a strained voice.

Bryce held his friend at arm's length. Paul rarely smiled since the divorce proceedings began. His dark eyes were full of sadness. Did Bryce look like that now? He sure felt like it.

"I have to do this, Paul, for more reasons than you'll understand or I have time to explain. When it's over I'll tell you everything." He let Paul go, although he hated to. It was such a relief to be with someone he could trust implicitly. But he couldn't unburden on Paul now.

Looking past Paul, Bryce noted the children's toys on the floor. "Your kids were here?"

"*Are* here," Paul said with satisfaction. "They're spending the night. As much as I miss Pam, I think I miss them more." Paul's eyes darkened with despair and other gloomy emotions. "She was the best thing in my life and I threw it away."

Paul had had it all, everything Bryce wanted, and it hadn't been enough. Some men didn't know when they had it made. Now Paul did. And, after this weekend, so did Bryce.

Bryce handed the manila envelope to Paul. "I want you to put this someplace safe. If anything happens to me, I've written a phone number and names on it. You're to call them. They're FBI."

Paul gripped Bryce's arms. "If you're in danger, why not let the FBI protect you?"

"It's complicated. Promise me you'll call them if anything happens to me."

"Damn it, Bryce!" Paul's face twisted. "I promise."

"Good. Don't tell anyone about the package. *Anyone.* I have to go."

"You can stay here where it's safe," Paul protested.

"I can't, but we'll get together soon and I'll tell you everything." Bryce prayed it would be so.

As he drove home his muscles tensed. A new bodyguard would be waiting for him. Bryce was sure if the man were a traitor he wouldn't just shoot Bryce on sight. That would tell Steele immediately who the traitor was. No, it would be something subtler, something indirect.

Bryce saw the dark sedan parked in front of his house when he drove up. The man inside nodded to him and Bryce relaxed a little. He'd been so focused on the bodyguard issue he hadn't thought about the bomber still out there, that it could be anyone.

As he pulled up to the garage, his new bodyguard appeared at his car window. Bryce rolled it down.

"I'm Smith. Mr. Steele sent me." He had short brown hair, brown eyes, and was of medium height and medium build. He had nondescript nailed.

"Thanks for coming. I appreciate Mr. Steele doing this for me."

"I've swept the grounds and found nothing suspicious. I waited for your arrival to check the house." Meaning he could easily have gotten in without a key. "I'd like you to wait in the car with the doors locked while I go inside."

After a tense ten minutes, Smith rapped on the car window and nearly gave Bryce a heart attack. Bryce took several deep breaths as he rolled down the window again.

"All clear. Put the car in the garage. I'll sweep it tomorrow before we leave."

Bryce did as he was told, then carried the first load into the house. Smith followed him, keeping alert, but making no sound when he moved. Inside the door Bryce switched on the inside and outside lights. He felt twitchy, as though the bomber lurked in the shadows or a bomb could be connected to any switch, despite Smith's assertions the place was clear.

By the time Bryce unloaded the car and locked the garage, it was fully dark outside. There was another twelve hours until Steele's trial began. Bryce needed rest but his muscles were so tense he was sure he couldn't fall asleep. He took a long, hot shower, washing off Ciara's scent, and tried to blank his mind. He'd never see her again. Her spying job was finished. He was once again the uncontested king of his house and his office.

Damn it, in two short days he'd gotten used to showering with someone else, to having Ciara wash his back and his intimate parts, to washing all her delectable parts, to the shower being a sexual place.

He had a damn hard-on again for a woman who'd betrayed him. How sick was that? Sure, she didn't work for Steele. That was some measure of relief. But she'd still spied on Bryce thinking he was corrupt. She'd lied to him. He'd never had casual sex, couldn't bring himself to, not with his trust issues. So why did he still want Ciara, knowing she didn't want him in return? He was a job to her.

Bryce turned off the water and leaned his hands against the tiles, letting his head hang down between them. A woman could fake orgasm, but Ciara hadn't. He'd felt her inner muscles milking him nearly a dozen times. A professional hooker might be able to force herself to have that many orgasms with a man who was just a job, but could a woman who worked for the Attorney General? If Ciara had been a woman who slept around, Bryce could see the AG choosing her to seduce him, but she had seemed like an old-fashioned girl—she certainly came from an old-fashioned family.

So what did it mean that her breasts peaked with arousal when he was near, that she was wet for him whenever he touched between her legs, that she kissed him like she was starving, that she rode him like she was desperate to be one with him?

God, did she really want him? It couldn't be true. He was her assignment. But nobody's body could lie that well, not for two whole days. Hope flooded painfully into his heart.

So she wanted him, so what? Her job was done. Did he think she'd drive to Detroit to . . . what? Give him regular sex? He shook his head and climbed out of the shower. He didn't think that at all. She wasn't that kind of woman.

Bryce scoffed and dried himself off. He had no idea what kind of woman Ciara was, what she would or wouldn't do.

He paused naked beside his perfectly made bed, such a contrast to how he'd left the bed at Ciara's house, and knew his last thought wasn't true. He knew a lot about Ciara. She loved her family. She donated time to teen basketball. She worked for a public agency whose purpose was to right consumer wrongs. She took pains with her appearance, she kept healthy and active, she didn't smoke or drink, rarely swore, and she was his perfect match in bed. She was his perfect match period.

Bryce didn't think he could lie in his bed alone and get any sleep, even though they'd never made love here. He knew the ache in his chest wouldn't go away nor the ache in his body.

There was no use thinking about Ciara. He couldn't do anything about their mutual attraction until the Steele case was over and it might drag on for months. By then it might be too late to find out if she returned his feelings. She might have found someone else.

His mood souring further, Bryce threw on shorts and a University of Michigan T-shirt and headed barefoot to his office. Until he got tired enough to sleep—if he did—he had a trial to prepare for. Work had been his passion before Ciara; it would have to suffice once more.

CHAPTER 19

Security at the courthouse was virgin tight. Bryce had to pass through the metal detector and the x-ray machine at the main entrance plus the cops had handheld metal detectors at the court-room doors. Smith remained vigilant, despite visible security measures. He wasn't armed, but Bryce had no doubt Smith knew numerous methods of lethal force.

As early as Bryce arrived, eager spectators and reporters had beaten him there. He ignored them and headed for the defense table. Smith sat directly behind him in the gallery. Bryce laid out his files and re-read his notes.

He felt hyperaware. He'd finally fallen asleep around three and gotten three hours of sleep. Two cups of coffee hadn't been enough, but he hadn't wanted to be jittery. The empty second chair mocked him. That's where Ciara would have sat. But the AG's underling couldn't defend a mobster. Bryce wondered what she would have done if he hadn't found out the truth. He was surprised she'd helped him at all, knowing who she really was. Not just helped, but succeeded in building a defense.

Had Bryce known who she really was, they could have worked together, not at cross-purposes. Another regret to file away for later.

Five minutes before nine Steele arrived, surrounded by news cameras and his big bodyguard. The courtroom was packed and noisy. Bryce rose to greet his client.

"Mr. Steele."

"Mr. Gannon. Ready to acquit me?"

"Yes, sir."

"Good. Where's your lovely assistant?"

"You know I try cases alone."

As Steele settled into his seat, his bodyguard sat beside Smith.

At nine the bailiff announced, "All rise. Court is now in session. The honorable Andy Garcia presiding."

Judge Garcia strode in wearing his black robe and took his seat. As Bryce sat back down, he saw a flash of red in his peripheral vision. Turning slightly, he spotted Ciara wearing a black V-neck knit top and a multi strand red necklace and matching earrings with her hair pulled up and back. Her loveliness struck him breathless and made his heart pound. She met his eyes for an endless moment, but he couldn't read them. The desire to be near her roared through his veins; it made him ache. He batted it down, fighting to focus as the judge prompted the U.S. Attorney to give his opening statement. Why was she here?

"The government will prove that Adam Steele is guilty of racketeering under the Racketeer Influenced and Corrupt Organizations Act, having committed fifteen federal crimes over the past three years including protection schemes, fraud, money laundering, extortion, and dealing in controlled substances. The government will prove each count in the indictment that Adam Steele has a pattern of racketeering. We will provide witnesses and testimony documenting his crimes and showing beyond a shadow of a doubt his lack of conscience, his lack of rectitude and his disdain of the laws of the United States."

As the U.S. Attorney droned on, Ciara again drew Bryce's gaze. He'd felt dead and alone without her. Now just her presence made him feel alive again. Had Baisden sent her? Did they still have doubts about him?

His gaze jerked to the front again as the bailiff handed Judge Garcia a note.

When Garcia's dark gaze met his, Bryce's whole body went cold. *Oh shit.*

Garcia leaned into the microphone. "I'm sorry, Counselor. Ladies and gentlemen, there's been a bomb threat—"

Several women screamed.

"Please exit the courthouse as swiftly as possible . . . " People rising and stampeding to the door drowned out the rest of his words.

Bryce quickly began to scoop his files and papers into his briefcase. He tried to maintain a calm facade while inside his mind was screaming for him to move. His pulse was a runaway train.

Smith came to his side. "Mr. Gannon, we need to leave."

"I'm not leaving these behind. It's Mr. Steele's defense." With a quick glance around he noted that Steele and his bodyguard had already left.

"Bryce, get out of here!" Ciara yelled from behind him.

His pulse leaped into his throat. She was in danger! He jammed the last bunch of files in the briefcase and swung into the gallery. Smith kept pace with him. They were the last people in line.

Bryce spotted Ciara outside the courtroom, but as he took a step towards her, arms roughly grabbed him and pulled. He jerked around ready to fight, only to face agents Pollack and Garrison.

"Move!" Garrison ordered. "You're exposed here."

Smith suddenly had a gun in his hand pointed at Garrison.

"FBI, dickhead," Pollack snarled flashing his badge. "Back off."

Garrison levered his gun at Smith.

Smith's cold eyes flickered, and then he lowered his gun.

Garrison kept his gun pointed at Smith. "You can report to Steele that Mr. Gannon is in our safekeeping until the bomb squad reports an all clear."

Smith backed away. "Mr. Steele won't like it. I'll be here when court resumes."

Bryce desperately searched for Ciara, but she was gone. The two Feds pulled him down a flight of stairs and out a side entrance to an unmarked white van, covering him with their bodies.

As they piled in, Pollack yelled, "Go!"

The van's tires squealed as it sped off.

"I'm glad to see you two," Bryce gasped.

"We assumed there'd be trouble and made a contingency plan," Pollack explained.

"Smart man. Where are we going?"

"Not far but someplace safe."

Minutes later, after much turning and backtracking, the van pulled up to a multi-story downtown apartment building.

"Let me get the door open, then get inside fast. But act natural once you're inside," Garrison instructed.

Garrison climbed out of the van, swiped his security card at the front door and as soon as it was open Bryce darted from the van to the lobby. It was one of the newly renovated downtown buildings with a tile foyer.

Garrison pressed the elevator button, and when it came, he, Bryce, and Pollack rode up to the third floor.

"Is this your safe house?" Bryce asked.

"No. Friend of a friend owns it," Garrison answered. "He's out of town."

It turned out to be a comfortable two-bedroom apartment done in a modern scheme. A little too much chrome for Bryce's taste, but the leather chair looked buttery soft. He took off his jacket and sank gratefully into it.

"How long do you think it will take?" Bryce asked.

Garrison was foraging in the fridge.

Pollack checked the windows. "I wouldn't expect to go back until after lunch. With your recent history, they're taking no chances." His cell chimed quietly and he answered it. "Yeah?" His brows pulled together in a fierce frown and he moved down the hall.

"Want a soda or something?" Garrison asked.

"Does this friend of a friend want you rummaging in his fridge?"

Garrison smiled like a barracuda. "Yep."

"Is there a Coke in there?"

Garrison brought him a can. Bryce popped the tab and gratefully took a swig, realizing he felt safe for the first time since Ciara's condo. Funny that he'd felt safe with her despite thinking she worked for Steele.

Pollack walked back into the room pocketing his phone. "There was a shooter on a rooftop across from the courthouse. It was a setup to flush you out into the open. He's dead though. Resisted arrest."

Bryce shivered with cold. But for the quick thinking of these men he'd be dead. "Is he part of Steele's organization?"

"We're checking."

"Thanks for saving my life."

"You could thank us by turning States' evidence. Give us that envelope your friend has."

"Soon." Bryce took a deep breath and a chance. They'd saved his life. He could trust them. "I'm going to try to get Steele convicted without him realizing what I'm doing."

The Feds' eyes widened. Garrison sat down with a plop on the leather sofa. "He'll kill you if he suspects."

"I know. The U.S. Attorney only needs two counts to convict. If I don't discredit two counts, I lose the case."

"But when was the last time you lost a case?" Pollack asked.

"It's been a while," Bryce admitted.

"So you don't think Steele will recognize a mediocre performance?"

"I didn't say it'd be easy or foolproof. I just wanted someone to know what I was trying to do, you know, in case. The items in the envelope would make it easier to convict Steele, but then it would be obvious I wanted to lose."

"All you have to do is ask for witness protection," Garrison said. "You don't have to risk your life where there's no guarantee."

"I have to do this. This is my last defense. I'm done either way."

"My God." Pollack sat in the other leather chair. "You're trying to be a damn hero."

"No. I didn't become a lawyer to defend scum like Steele. I don't know how I got on this road. This is the only way I know to find my way back."

Garrison nodded. "That's good enough for me." He raised his Coke in a toast.

Pollack added, "We'll do what we can to keep you alive so you can do your thing. I think it's sheer suicide though."

"Life is risky business," Bryce replied. Only he hadn't taken a risk since college. Not until Ciara.

• • •

Where was Bryce? Ciara paced her hotel room. They'd sent everyone from the visitor's gallery home with a phone number to call to let them know when trial would resume. She'd called it five times already only to hear the recording to call back later.

She'd nearly screamed when the two men grabbed Bryce outside the courtroom until she'd recognized the FBI agents. Then there'd almost been a gun battle with the man she assumed was Bryce's bodyguard.

It had been two hours. Was Bryce safe? Had the FBI gotten him away without an incident? She had the TV tuned to a local station. Other than a brief report of the bomb threat repeated on all the local networks, the stations had returned to regular daytime programming.

Ciara wrapped her arms around herself, pressing them against her aching breasts. Her whole body ached to be held in Bryce's arms. She felt sick with worry for him. She wanted to beg his forgiveness for spying on him, for lying to him, for doubting him. If he could forgive her, she'd do everything in her power to win his trust. Whatever it took for as long as it took.

He needed her and she needed him. He made her feel alive, challenged yet safe. He was a man like her brother-in-law Esteban, a man who could be trusted, a man who when he committed to a woman would give her his all.

She had Bryce's complete attention. She'd broken through his cool veneer. He'd looked shocked to see her in court, not angry or hostile. His gaze had been almost hungry. She was sure he felt the need that she felt now. They'd made promises that had gone unfulfilled. They weren't done with one another.

And Bryce had to stay alive so they could finish what they'd started . . . if it took the rest of their lives.

Her cell rang and she snatched it from the counter. It was the attorney general. "Talk to me."

"The FBI killed a rooftop sniper staking out the courthouse. They're keeping it under wraps for now."

Ciara's breath whooshed out and she sank into a kitchen chair. She felt lightheaded. "Is Bryce all right?"

"Gannon and the Feds are off the radar. I've been on the phone with the U.S. Attorney. He's going to delve into police corruption in Detroit when this is over. If the agents who took Gannon can be trusted—"

"I think they can."

"Then they don't trust their own to say where they've got Gannon stashed."

"God, everybody's gunning for Bryce. We've got to help him!"

"It gets worse. Bombers don't normally become shooters. So I think the bomber is still out there. It could be that Steele's rival is sending in different types of hitters. But the bomber seems focused. I think he'll try again."

Helpless rage curled Ciara's hands into fists. She needed to protect Bryce. She wanted this faceless bomber stopped, but she had no training in threat prevention, no skill with guns or explosives. What could she do other than throw herself between Bryce and danger? But she didn't want to die.

"I wish you weren't in the danger zone," he said.

"I wish none of us were. Thanks for the info."

In half an hour she found out court would resume at one-thirty. She'd see Bryce in a few hours. She prayed wherever the agents had him stashed they'd keep him safe. And that they'd get him to the courtroom safely. Steele's people and the bomber would be watching for his return. So would she.

CHAPTER 20

Bryce was safe! Ciara felt such relief when she saw him flanked by the two FBI agents that she would have fallen had she not been seated. She ate him up with her eyes—his cold, almost hauteur demeanor; the perfection of his navy suit with the ever-present white shirt, the ruthlessly controlled hair.

His gaze snagged hers and clung. Her body heated to a melting point, her heart raced, and her breathing hitched. She needed to be alone with him in the worst way. His gaze spoke volumes, and yet he only said one word in passing.

"Ciara."

"Bryce." Did he hear the neediness in her voice, the apology—the regret?

The FBI agents faded to the walls. Bryce shook hands with Steele. They spoke in low tones. Both men looked equally cold, yet Ciara felt Steele was cold to the core, while Bryce had a core of hot passion.

A caramel-colored suit cut off Ciara's view of Bryce. She waited for the person to sit down, but they continued blocking her view as they moved towards the front. The suit resolved itself into perfect curves, perfect legs, and perfect blonde hair. Ciara felt irritated at seeing Monique Dennison here. She seemed to be everywhere they went. Ciara hadn't realized Bryce and Monique moved in the same circles but she should have. They'd dated for a year. All the gossip rags thought the two would marry because they seemed so suited.

Jealousy licked at Ciara. What she and Bryce had done together—those marvelous matings—he'd done those things with the perfect blonde.

Monique caught Bryce's attention. For a moment he looked irritated, then his face smoothed covering his emotions.

Ciara felt a spurt of glee. Bryce didn't want to see Monique. She wasn't so perfect after all. In fact, that ugly black purse looked hideous with the tight suit. Ciara had thought the woman had better taste than that.

Monique unzipped the dreadful purse. Then she adjusted the open bag in front of her as she moved through the swinging gallery gate.

Every alarm in Ciara's body went off. She catapulted to her feet, her heart thundering. Unfortunately, her movement drew Bryce's startled gaze to her and away from Monique. Ciara hurtled forward. She had to be in time! She saw the bodyguards' gazes snap to her, but they'd be too slow.

She was a giant leap away when she screamed, "Bryce, get down!"

Monique was lifting the purse and turning when Ciara's palms slammed into her back with the force of her five-foot-ten muscle behind them. Bryce dived to the right as Ciara shoved Monique to the left. As she fell, Monique knocked down Adam Steele, like dominoes tumbling. White powder exploded into the air in a high rooster tail circling up and over Monique and forward over Steele. Ricin!

Ciara held her breath as she skidded to a stop. Then she lost her balance and fell on her butt. The cloud of white powder was spreading outward over her legs as someone grabbed Ciara's arm and dragged her backwards.

"Ciara!"

Bryce! Oh God. Ciara turned towards him. "Bryce, it's ricin! Don't inhale it!" she shrieked, fear for him overcoming all else. But he continued to drag her clear.

Women's screams filled the courtroom. Bodies were in motion. It was a contest between the people trying to get out of the courtroom and those trying to reach the front.

Adam Steele lay on his back, gasping, his face covered with a thick coating of white powder.

Monique lay face down in the white powder. Her blonde hair and the back of her suit were white. She screamed, "You bitch!" Then huge racking coughs claimed her.

Ciara saw agent Garrison step forward, a phone in his hand. Bryce's bodyguard and Steele's big bodyguard leaned forward towards Steele.

"Get back!" she screamed. "It's ricin. It's a lethal poison! Don't breathe it in!"

Garrison and the spectators around them jerked back. The bodyguards looked down at their gasping boss. Monique's body spasmed. Ciara was pretty sure Monique was dying, but there was nothing Ciara could do to help until the white mist settled. She didn't know how much ricin contaminated her, but there were white spots on her left arm and hand, and on her skirt as high as her hips. She didn't know if she'd breathed any in when she screamed at Bryce or the Feds.

"Bryce, get back. I don't want you exposed to this."

He held on tighter. She'd have a bruise on her bicep. "If I lose you, I'd rather go too." He sounded slightly winded.

Ciara gave him an exasperated look. "Bryce, you fool, I have no intention of dying. I have some major apologizing to do and then you and I made some promises we haven't kept yet."

He went completely still. "Apologies? Promises?"

"Yeah. Now move where it's safe."

"Yes, Counselor." He rose and moved to stand with the U.S. Attorney. He took out his inhaler and used it.

Ciara stared at him for one long, hungry moment. He looked a little rumpled, but she didn't see any white powder on him, thank God. Then she turned back to the victims. Monique lay still. Steele's breathing had slowed. Each breath was a noisy struggle. Was this what Bryce had looked like when he'd received the letter bomb? It was hideous to watch. And then the sound stopped. Steele's chest ceased moving. His huge bodyguard looked down in horror. The other man, Bryce's bodyguard, lifted his head and slowly smiled at Ciara. With two fingers he gave her a mock solute, turned, and walked away.

The rival! Oh, God. The man worked for Steele's rival. He'd been alone with Bryce last night, probably frustrated that he couldn't kill Bryce without Steele knowing who did it. Earlier today he would have herded Bryce out to the sniper. Her breaths came fast like she'd been running.

Ciara looked at Steele again. God, that could have been Bryce! Had Ciara not acted as quickly as she had things might have been horribly different. Tears blurred her eyes. She turned to Bryce as to a lodestone. His lips pursed as he glanced at Steele and spoke to the U.S. Attorney.

Then he approached and hunkered down a few feet from her. "Don't cry. You saved me."

"I had to. I think I love you."

His face worked. "Thank God, because I know I love you."

Ciara felt her heart expand like the Grinch in the Dr. Seuss tale. "I don't want to lose you, Bryce, ever. I want to spend the rest of my life telling you how much I want you."

Pollack squatted down next to Bryce. "Nine-one-one responders will be here in a minute." He looked at Steele. "Good work, Miss Alafita."

Ciara began to cry in earnest. She'd killed two people. She hadn't intended to, but they were dead all the same. She hissed at Bryce when he reached for her and he drew back.

"That man, your bodyguard, he worked for Steele's rival. He would have killed you."

"How do you know?" Pollack demanded.

"He smiled at me. He saluted me. Goal achieved."

"Then you're safe, Gannon. They've got no reason to come after you now. He'll report to his boss that Steele's dead."

Bryce nodded. "Good, because I'm tired of crowds around me. I want my life back."

Ciara blubbered, "I don't want to be sick."

"I'll be there with you," Bryce promised. "Every minute. From now on."

"Bryce, I don't want to spend the night in the hospital. I want to spend it with you."

Pollack looked from Ciara to Bryce and backed away in a hurry, already raising his phone to his mouth.

"We won't have to sleep alone ever again, okay?" Bryce said.

She nodded. "Promise?"

"I do."

"Good."

The EMTs arrived in biohazard suits and that severed her conversation with Bryce. But they'd said amazing things to each other. She hoped there'd be time to say the rest. A lifetime.

CHAPTER 21

Bryce fitted Ciara's nude body against him in his bed. He'd never been so frightened as when the ricin flew into the air in front of her. That she'd managed to avoid inhaling any of it while he pulled her free amazed him. She said she'd held her breath. She was a very smart woman. She'd realized Monique meant to harm him, and she'd risked her life to protect him.

Agents Pollack and Garrison had found printed directions for making ricin and letter bombs in Monique's condo. Bryce had spent a year with her and never realized she had a vicious nature. She didn't like losing. It was now obvious she didn't want to break up with him. She must have thought he'd change his mind about seeking a judgeship if she left him. When he didn't, she decided if she couldn't have him, no one could. He shuddered. He could have died before he knew the love that now rested in his arms.

"You're all tense again," Ciara complained from his shoulder.

Bryce leaned down and kissed her long and hard. "I could have lost you."

She hugged him. "And I could have lost you."

"But you protected me."

"I had to. I wanted you for myself."

He chuckled. "You had me." He nodded to their cooling bodies.

"That was hardly want. Give me a minute and I'll show you real want."

"I can't wait. Ciara—"

She pressed her finger to his lips. "I know. I betrayed you. I'm sorry. I won't ever do it again."

Bryce removed her finger. "Apology accepted. Will you marry me?" The words slipped out, but they felt right.

Ciara inhaled. "Don't you need time to be sure? I mean, I live in Lansing. You live here."

"I'm giving up my practice. I don't want to do that kind of work anymore. I thought I'd move to Lansing, give your mother a break from playing matchmaker."

"And what, become a kept man?" Ciara playfully whacked his arm. "Fool. I was looking forward to joining your practice as a full partner. Gannon and Alafita."

"Gannon and Gannon, you mean." Bryce sighed. "I'm tired of defending the bad guys."

Ciara lifted her head. "Who says we have to? Since you want to be a judge, you probably should turn over a new leaf."

"If I become a judge, I'd have to leave the practice anyway."

"Maybe we'll have a child by then and I can stay home and play mommy for a while." She looked dreamy.

He smiled. He wanted that too. "You're getting ahead of yourself, Ciara. You haven't even said yes yet."

"Yes!"

They sealed their contract with a kiss.

More from This Author

(From *Touchpoint*)

The building looked like it had suffered a terrorist attack, only it hadn't. Christian Ziko, standing in front of it, looked like any other man, but he wasn't. He was the architect of this destruction and Gabrielle Healey was going to prove it.

The Densmore Building had been a dazzling jewel in the crown of Detroit's revitalized downtown waterfront. The glass third floor jutting out into the atrium with no visible means of support was an impressive engineering marvel. That floor was chosen for the hottest new disco in town.

It became a deathtrap when part of it collapsed, shattering the glass walls and hurling unsuspecting dancers over the edge. Six people were killed and a dozen others injured.

Gabrielle hadn't expected to see Ziko here, since he'd disappeared shortly after the collapse. She thought he might be ashamed or afraid to show his face in public. He should be. With his black hair and dressed all in black, he looked like the cold-blooded killer some thought him to be. Before the Densmore, he'd been touted as a brilliant and innovative architect for his radical designs. Now one local newspaper called him "the architect of death." She wanted to hate him. How dare he create a design so flawed it didn't hold up for six months after it was built?

But she couldn't allow herself to become emotionally involved in her investigation. Her job wasn't to pass judgment, but to gather facts to protect her employer, Michigan Casualty, that had insured the building, from having to pay a claim. Her team had ruled out everything but the architect's design. All she needed was proof to condemn Ziko.

She had so many questions to ask him, and here was the perfect opportunity.

Stepping from the shadows of the building, her sneaker sent a stone skittering across the pavement, announcing her to Ziko. When he turned to face her, she sucked in her breath at what she saw. Lines of strain bracketed his tight mouth and a deep furrow beetled his black brows. But what struck her like a blow was the pain in his Caribbean blue eyes. She almost cried out just looking into their tortured depths.

She'd expected to find a cold, heartless bastard, but tearing pain didn't make any sense. He'd made one public apology . . . and then remained glaringly silent. He hadn't faced the grieving families, or visited the injured in the hospital, or been on-site during the investigation.

Gabrielle had to touch him. Her clairvoyance allowed her to glean information about a person or object through physical contact. It helped her perform her job as an insurance investigator exceptionally well. But Ziko made her uneasy. There was a darkness about him that had nothing to do with his black jeans and T-shirt. His tee clung to muscled biceps and a firm chest. Her feminine instincts sat up and howled their notice.

She shook off her fanciful thoughts and the unwanted attraction. She was here to do a job, and Christian Ziko could provide the truth.

Taking a cleansing breath, she held out her hand as she moved toward him. "Mr. Ziko? I'm Gabrielle Healey from Michigan Casualty."

At the first touch of his surprisingly cool skin, a picture formed in Gabrielle's mind, clear in the center but fuzzy around the edges. *Christian Ziko sat hunched over his drawing board, his pencil meticulously detailing on the paper tacked to it. It was a drawing of the Densmore and his blue eyes were soft with what could only be described as love as he worked on it. There was joy in his movements, in the light way he held his pencil, and in his bare toes gripping the bottom rung of his wooden stool.*

Gabrielle tore herself away from Ziko and the vision disappeared. She felt shaken by a kernel of doubt. He'd loved it? Then how could he have designed it so poorly?

"Do I know you?" he asked.

"No. Michigan Casualty insured the building. I'm investigating the collapse."

His face closed up and his lips flatlined. "Oh. Well, I'm glad there's insurance money to make repairs."

"Unless they have to tear the building down. The building inspectors have to decide if the Densmore is structurally sound. But I'm not telling you anything you don't already know."

But she was. She could see it as the color leeched from his face, leaving the lines of strain etched starkly into his skin. What the hell?

"I wasn't aware of that," he said.

Where had he been that he hadn't kept up with the TV, newspaper, and radio coverage? "Have you been out of town?" That would explain his absence from the public eye.

He studied the derelict building, his jaw muscles bunching, for so long she thought he didn't intend to answer. Finally one word came out, although reluctantly. "Yes." It was a word full of anger and some other dark emotion. Tension resonated from him. Wherever he'd been, it hadn't relaxed him.

Gabrielle wanted to touch him again to get a picture of what he'd been doing during that time, but she didn't want any more doubts.

Oddly enough, the word that described his present state was vulnerable, as though he was affected by what had happened.

But that was crazy. Ziko's lack of public response showed his unconcern.

"I won't keep you from your work." He made a half turn away from her.

"Wait. Let me give you my card in case you need to contact me." She dug in her purse.

"I won't need to—"

"Here," she interrupted, thrusting a card at him. For some reason, it seemed imperative he have a way to contact her.

His hand brushed hers as he took the card and another vision blasted to life in her mind. *A cop slammed Ziko face first against a painted wall. As Ziko tried to rear back, the policeman jammed his billy club against Ziko's neck.*

"I'm innocent!" The wall muffled his shout.

"Tell it to the judge," the cop growled.

Another policeman moved behind Ziko and roughly cuffed him.

Gabrielle jerked back from him, unable to deal with the tumult of emotions the vision caused. This was a precognitive vision, more rare for her. It showed one possible future, if nothing changed between now and then. She was sure she had something to do with this future coming true, but whether it was due to action or inaction, she didn't know.

Ziko headed toward the front door of the Densmore.

"Did your building collapse because of something you did, or was it an accident?" She aimed the words at his back.

• • •

Christian flinched. Since the press had already slandered his name and reputation, he'd expected her question, but it hurt to hear her accusation. He didn't think he would get used to strangers hating him for something he'd supposedly done, and for some reason it felt worse coming from her.

He turned, the denial automatic. "No."

Then guilt swamped him. Maybe it was his fault. If he hadn't been working on half a dozen projects at once, he would have caught whatever error created this disaster. He cursed himself for not being on-site during construction. Doubt crept in and gnawed at his gut. How could something he'd designed fail?

When he added, "It couldn't have been my fault," even he heard the uncertainty in his voice.

Gabrielle frowned, her gently arched black brows pulling together. "You don't sound certain."

Christian's fists clenched at his side. "Something terrible happened to this building, Ms. Healey. I don't know what, but I couldn't have done it. I build things, beautiful things. I don't destroy them."

"Some of the news reports said your arrogance killed those people, that you were too brash in your assurances the design would work."

There was something he was certain of. "DesignCorp tested my design. Mr. Densmore insisted on it because it was so radical. It withstood all their structural tests."

"Maybe it only worked in the lab."

Stung, he lifted his chin. "No, it should have held up."

She waved toward the building. "Clearly it didn't. A man whose sister died when she fell from the third floor wants you tried for murder."

Someone else hated him. "I didn't know that."

Gabrielle's blue eyes narrowed. "Hasn't anyone kept you up-to-date, forwarded you the news?"

"No." News upset the residents at the Crittenden facility, so medical management blocked it. And his brother Paul hadn't told him any of it, although Christian had been too drugged to care if Paul had.

How had everything gone so wrong that he was considered a worse person in this town than Osama bin Laden? He'd believed the newspapers and magazines when they'd called him the Golden Boy of Architecture. His head had swelled with their praise over his work. Now he was accused of murder. No one seemed interested in proving his innocence, only in exhorting his guilt. Even this woman, who, in her capacity as an investigator, had the power to destroy him.

Gabrielle Healey was a striking woman. Her straight black hair and high cheekbones hinted at a Native American heritage. Her wide-spaced blue eyes were full of intelligence and incisive questions that might probe too deeply. Yet her full lips offered a sensuality he wanted to explore. She was a dangerous combination. She was an investigator and he had things to hide. Things like Crittenden and the reason he'd gone there.

If only she was on his side, she could use that intense mental focus to help him find out what went wrong with the Densmore and prove to everyone's satisfaction he wasn't at fault. Clearly, if he wanted to prove his innocence, he'd have to do his own investigation. He owed it to the dead and to himself to find out.

Gabrielle interrupted his thoughts. "I'd like to ask you some questions."

"I really don't have time." He was afraid what she'd ask, what he might admit accidentally, and what she'd read into anything he said.

She pounced anyway. "Do you have something to hide?"

Yes, he wanted to shout, a mental illness. But he couldn't do that because bipolar disorder had a negative stigma attached to it. It was feared and scorned and misunderstood. And since he'd been at Crittenden, he couldn't afford for anyone to find out, because if they did, they'd blame the Densmore's collapse on it. Just like this woman would.

Instead, he said, "I don't see how I can help you with your investigation."

"Who better than the architect? What can it hurt to walk through the wreckage with me?"

That was a loaded question. Walking through it the first time had caused horrific nightmares and his spiral into a depression that got him committed to Crittenden. He'd been released only a few hours ago and had no intention of going back. He should avoid a repeat performance by steering clear of the interior.

Then why the hell was he here? If he was going to take on the task of clearing his name, he had to go inside. By now, the chalk outlines were probably gone. He hoped the bloodstains had been cleaned up.

"Yeah, let's go inside." He hoped she couldn't hear the trepidation in his voice caused by his belly quivering with nerves.

Gabrielle stopped at the entrance and unlocked the padlock which held the doors chained shut. Christian hadn't even noticed the chain. He couldn't have gotten inside if he'd wanted to.

The interior was dim with so many windows boarded up. It smelled of dust and disuse . . . and death. Lights high up in the ceiling and along the brick walls came on, lighting his personal nightmare. Steel girders still hung exposed from the third floor structure, looking like at any moment they'd tear loose and catapult into the remaining unbroken panes of glass. One girder lay across the lobby floor like a huge forgotten piece of erector set. Part of the glass ceiling had been replaced by plywood.

This building had been his vision from the moment he first heard Charles Densmore speak about creating a tribute to his late wife. Christian had slaved over draft after draft trying to create a masterpiece of air and light, and he'd thought he had. Somehow his dream had turned into a nightmare. What was left was dreary ruin, the death of his dream.

"Mr. Ziko?"

Christian had a feeling Gabrielle had called his name more than once, but he hadn't heard her. "What?"

"Are you all right?"

"I'm fine." It was a lie, but at least his voice was steady when he said it.

"What do you see?"

"The same thing you do—devastating destruction. This place was beautiful when it was completed." He remembered entering the Densmore for the grand opening. The guests had been awed by the seemingly unsupported third floor overhang. It had been a glittering spectacle that night. Now it more closely resembled a derelict from the ghettos of Detroit.

"Sometimes beauty masks something darker," she said.

"No. I designed it in Mrs. Densmore's memory. She wouldn't have wanted this." A sweep of his hand indicated the current state.

"You're human. You made a mistake."

He looked into her inquisitive blue eyes. She wanted answers, but was there judgment under the intelligent probe? He didn't know. "I thought a man was innocent until proven guilty."

She stiffened and he felt guilty because he'd lashed out.

"So you're alleging you're innocent?"

"It doesn't matter what I say if you've already made up your mind." But it did matter, a lot more than it should have.

"Believe it or not, I'm looking for the truth. However, I do know what the prevailing opinion is."

If only he could sway this one person . . . but "if onlys" were for dreamers. If only he could go back in time and be on-site during construction, he'd prevent this whole calamity. He looked away from her intriguing face to the wreckage, from one torment to another.

This was his responsibility. He'd designed the Densmore. On paper, he was intimately familiar with every nook and cranny of the building. He was the best hope of finding out why it failed. And if he found he was at fault . . . well, he'd cross that bridge when he came to it.

In the mood for more Crimson Romance?
Check out *The Way You Love Me*
by Janis Lee Thereault
at *CrimsonRomance.com.*